Foggage

PATRICK MCGINLEY was born in Donegal in 1937 and was educated at Galway University. He spent four years teaching in Ireland before taking up a career in publishing in London. He now lives in Kent with his family but regularly returns to Donegal in the Irish Midlands.

His previous novels are *Fox Prints*, *Goosefoot*, which is also available in Flamingo, and *Bogmail*, which will be published in Flamingo in 1986.

Patrick McGinley

Foggage

FLAMINGO

Published by Fontana Paperbacks

First published in Great Britain
by Jonathan Cape Ltd 1984

This Flamingo edition first published
in 1985 by Fontana Paperbacks,
8 Grafton Street, London W1X 3LA

Flamingo is an imprint of
Fontana Paperbacks, a division
of the Collins Publishing Group

Made and printed in Great Britain by
William Collins Sons & Co. Ltd, Glasgow

To Kathleen

My name is Death: the last best friend am I.
ROBERT SOUTHEY

Part One

1

The January day was cold with a grey sky that seemed to rest on the hedge at the end of the unploughed field. Kevin Hurley was digging a drain. He was wrapped in a grey overcoat in the narrow tractor cab, a dirt-caked sack on the metal seat beneath him, tentacles of cold exploring his legs inside his mud-splashed Wellingtons. His father's legs were also cold, blue-veined shanks frozen stiff from toe to knee. Cold gripped the surrounding hedges and the small animals they sheltered, and the gap-toothed wind that came down from Slieve Bloom in the north broke twigs off trees and hissed at the loose door of the cab. The warmth of his life seemed to have evaporated forever. Summer and autumn had made way for winter, and yet he was only in his fortieth year. Cold weather, cold clothes, cold flesh, cold clay. His father would fail to wake from sleep one morning, and then he and Maureen would be alone.

A solitary crow rose over a hedge and dipped twice as it fled before a whirring tail wind. In this same field on a warm day of summer he had seen a bird he did not recognize pursued by a grey-glinting sparrow hawk. Something dropped from the bird's beak, the hawk swooped, and Kevin realized that the nameless bird had lost its fledgling. He himself lacked a fledgling; he had neither son nor daughter to meet him in the lane. When the time came, his farm would go to his younger sister's only son, little Breffny Kilgallon, who, because of his hothouse upbringing, would see it as collateral, not land.

He could bear the numbness in his toes no longer. He jumped out of the tractor and set off briskly for the Three Acres to check the earliest of his winter barley. A flock of cantankerous starlings descended like a shower of hail from the sky, settling noisily on the bare lea land with jerky movements. He detested starlings, the yobbos of the open fields. Luckily, they were small. He felt certain that if birds ever took over the planet, the starlings would be in the van of destruction. One of them pulled a long earthworm out of a poached track and flew into a hedge to consume it alone. Uncivilized buggers, they did not even trust one another.

At ten to one by his watch he returned to the tractor and drove home to dinner. As he swung into the rutted lane, a moulting hen, the picture of misery, dashed headlong in front of the wheels, and then he saw Pup lolloping towards him, his hindquarters slewing as if he were about to keel over. Pup was the silliest dog he had ever seen, good for nothing except chasing the hens. He had tried to train him on wet days, but all tutelage was lost on him. At first he had thought of calling him Bosco after all the other dogs he'd had at Clonglass, but when he discovered how stupid he was, he decided that to dignify him with a proper name would be unforgivable, that simple "Pup" was good enough for him.

The kitchen reeked warmly of boiled potatoes. His sister Maureen laid a platter of cold beef in the centre of the table and a plate of marrow-fat peas and steaming parsnips at the end where he usually sat. The peas were overdone, a glutinous mess, emitting a cloud of steam that mingled with that of the parsnips, making his nostrils twitch with the expectation of warmth and nourishment. As Maureen never troubled to lay the table, he went to the dresser and got out a worn knife and fork and a bread knife to carve the beef.

"Will you get me an onion?" he said, letting a large dollop of mustard fall on the edge of his plate.

She reached up, pulled on onion from the string above the range, and placed it beside the mustard pot.

"Go easy on the English, it's all we've got," she said. "I cycled down to Carroll's for more this morning, but all they had was French. And he told me they haven't got any in Killage either."

"French mustard's no good. I hope you didn't waste money on it."

"I only bought a six-ounce jar. I thought you might mix it with what's left of the English to make it less obnoxious-like to your lady's palate."

"You know bugger all about my palate," he grumbled as he peeled the onion. He was concerned about the lack of English mustard, so concerned that he had decided to drive eleven miles to Roscrea after dinner to stock up for the rest of the winter.

Maureen poured herself a mug of vegetable soup from the black saucepan and sat down beside him while he carved three thick slices of beef for her. She always made vegetable soup for dinner, thick, creamy soup with large cubes of carrot and turnip floating in it and an inch-deep layer of barley at the bottom. She never ate the soup before the main course; she drank it from the mug to wash down the meat and vegetables, making a sucking sound as she drained it before licking the barley off a teaspoon. As usual, she offered Kevin a mug, and as usual he refused with the comment that "for the workingman dry packing is best."

For a while they were silent. Kevin smeared the cold beef with mustard, peeled six good-sized potatoes, cut the raw onion into rings, and fell to. He liked potatoes and other vegetables, especially on winter days when the steam from them took the frost off his chin, but he liked beef more. A favourite saying of his was "Bacon is meat and so is mutton, but beef is beef." He killed his own beef, choosing for the knife the best bullock of the herd, and as he did so he told himself that he knew the joints as intimately as any butcher. The freezer in the dairy was always well stocked. They ate beef in various forms six days a week and pig's liver on Sunday. He bought the liver in Killage on Saturday evenings, and while other people were roasting their weekly joint on Sunday mornings, Maureen would fry the liver for dinner and, if any remained, again for tea.

His imagination was running so vividly on winter barley and the profit from last year's winter fattening that he had cleared his plate before he had time to take in the taste. He felt so cheated that he peeled another six potatoes and carved two more slices of beef. He would have carved three if he'd had enough mustard; a quick look in the pot had told him that he only had enough for two. When he had finished, Maureen said that the postman had brought a letter from Concepta, their younger sister, who was married to a bank manager in Roscrea. She had asked once again if Kevin had any intention of marrying and threatened to come to see them next week. Kevin detested Concepta even more than he detested her husband, so he peeled another potato and said nothing. Encouraged by his silence and fortified by the postman's gossip, Maureen began a roll call of the sick, the dying, and the newly dead. He listened with fortitude, noting her unerring ability to draw comfort from each separate piece of news, from illness as well as health, from death as well as life.

"Will you get me my beer?" he said when he had cleared his plate and she had finally paused for breath.

She went to the parlour and came back with a tumbler and a bottle of ale. He levered off the cap with his penknife and drank straight from the bottle so that the rising gas might tickle his nostrils. Maureen must have known all that by now, but she still placed a tumbler before him, and afterwards she would wash it, though he had not touched it. It was a womanly foible, he supposed, and as such it deserved acceptance if not respect.

"Will you be having your tea upstairs?" she asked.

"I'm going up to lie down," he replied without looking at her.

He pulled off his dirty Wellingtons and in stocking feet climbed the dark stairs and tiptoed down the corridor so as not to disturb their bedridden father. His sister's room was small and bare, with nothing between the walls except a double bed, a kitchen chair, and an old bureau with a statue of the Infant of Prague in the centre. He took off his trousers and underpants and jumped into her bed in his shirt and vest. It was freezing between the sheets, and he faced the wall and closed his eyes, wishing that he'd installed central heating when things were cheap. After a while Maureen came up with his tea and placed it on the chair beside the bed. Then she kicked off her unlaced shoes, drew the curtains, and slid into bed beside him. She put a muscular arm round his waist, pressed the tip of her chin into the back of his neck, and rubbed her hard mound against his bony backside. They lay in silence in the semidarkness while he waited for the sheets to thaw, and in his mind two images contended for supremacy—the white roots in the clay from the drain-digging and Maureen like a mischievous monkey on his back.

Maureen was the flickering flame that radiated what warmth he enjoyed in his life. She was his twin, a big handsome woman with a big freckled face, heavy udderlike breasts, thick thighs, and a bottom that overflowed the edge of the chair when she sat down. In that respect, she resembled her dead mother, who was also shapeless, with a stomach that spilled over the top of her steel-ribbed corset. Maureen was more sensuous than her mother, though. She had a wide mouth with big lips that became sweetly slippery when he kissed them, and though she wore loose dresses to conceal her figure, she only succeeded in betraying bulges in unexpected places whenever she stooped. She was an earthy girl, assiduous in bed and equally assiduous in the farmyard. She would shuffle about in wide unlaced shoes with splashes of slurry on her unstockinged calves, and when she stooped over a tub to mix the hens' feed she would place her flat feet apart, and her unkempt hair would hang down like thrums about her face. She never left the farm except to go shopping in Killage on Fridays and to accompany him to early Mass on Sunday mornings. The house and farmyard were her life, and if her horizons extended farther afield she had to thank the garrulous postman and Monsignor McGladdery, who came once a month with comfort and Communion for their senile father.

When their bodies had warmed the bedclothes, he turned round and embraced her. Her hair smelt of turf smoke from the range and her breath was warm and heavy like a cow's. He pulled up his shirt under his arms and then her dress, and they kissed mutely with legs entwined. He thought of a bull that is slow in service, and he told himself that if he did not hurry his tea would be cold. He had been doing it too often lately, more often than he thought good for him. He had done it on Monday and on Wednesday, and here he was doing it again on Friday. He was denying the Foggage Principle, which was first and foremost a principle of conservation. Maureen was ready, but his tardy blood still refused to rush to his sleeping member.

He recalled going to a wedding in London as a young man, a rampageous Irish wedding with fiddle music, drink, and dancing that horrified the lower-middle-class English neighbours, a wedding that filled him with intimations of sensuality and drove him to solitary masturbation in the roofless garden shed. He came back from Holyhead on the mail boat, and on the crowded train from Dun Laoghaire to Dublin a young girl came in and stood between his legs. She was wearing a long white dress that reminded him of a field of snow at dawn before man or beast has poached it. He wanted to get up and offer her his seat, but she really was too beautiful. Perhaps she was the kind of woman who would spurn his offer, a modern woman who thought herself stronger than any mortal man. Her legs, responding to the swaying of the train and the jolting of the wheels over points, caressed his knees while he counted the tucks in her dress below the belt. Coming into Westland Row, she raised her arm to grip the rack above his head, and he glimpsed her bra through the armhole of her dress—a soiled off-white bra with a hem that had been blackened by the sweat of long wear. The train stopped, the door opened, and she was gone. He scrambled out, but she had vanished. Like a vision, she had faded from sight, but he had not lost her. Again and again she returned to him on Saturday nights, when, after a few drinks, he would seek his bachelor bed for self-given solace before sleep. She would slip in beside him in her snow-bright dress, white and off-white, at once pure and defiled. Before he had known Maureen, she was his only woman, and she had kept him warm through many a midland winter. More important, she had now returned to help him in his need.

When he finally got under way, he did not indulge in fancy

meanderings, but went to the point with such directness that any woman except Maureen would have accused him of breaking and entering.

"Am I a good ride?" she whispered at the end of their abrupt but satisfying struggle.

"You mustn't ask me questions like that."

"Why?"

"It isn't right. It's tempting Providence," he said.

"There's no harm in that."

"Only old trollops think such thoughts."

"I want to know," she persisted.

"Well, you're asking the wrong man. You're the only woman I've ever lain with."

"You're not doing it just to please me?"

"I'm doing it to please myself. Now, does that satisfy you?" he said, sitting up in bed.

"Do you ever think about us?"

"No."

"I was thinking in bed this morning. I'll bet the neighbours see me as an old maid and you as a sapless bachelor. Little do they know that there's more heat in this house than in all the other houses of the townland put together."

She went to the window to pull back the curtains, and he drank his tea at a draught. He waited until she had gone downstairs, then got out of bed and examined his testicles. His little bag looked as it usually did, wrinkled and asymmetrical, and he weighed it in his hand, aware of the slight throb of pain inside it. For the past couple of weeks the pain always came after intercourse with Maureen; but perhaps it was one of those pains that come and go, like the pain he used to get in his rectum after masturbation with the girl in the off-white bra. When he went downstairs to the kitchen, Maureen poured him another cup of tea and he sat by the window, wondering if there was such a thing as cancer of the scrotum.

A loud thump above his head made him sit up.

"Did you give him his drink?" he asked Maureen.

"I did, before you came in."

His father was a bloody nuisance. He was senile now, with a childish but all-consuming ambition to outlive Donie Dunne, a once-litigious neighbour who was three years his junior. He was in the habit of telling everyone that he was ninety-nine, but Kevin knew from the birth certificate he had discovered inside the grandfather clock that he was only ninety-six. He lay in bed all day with a walking stick and a thermos flask of tea laced with whiskey on the table beside him, and whenever he felt in need of sustenance he took a swig of the tea and whenever he felt in need of attention he pounded the floor with the stick. He ate little now, only porridge in the morning followed by cup after cup of Bovril, and cubes of shop bread dunked in hot milk and sprinkled with sugar in the evening. The latter dish he called "goody," a word he had resurrected from his first childhood. He was full of fads. He would not take cow's milk in his tea because of his fear of brucellosis, and he insisted on storing the tins of condensed milk he used under the bedside table so that he could keep an eye on stocks. However, he insisted on having cow's milk with his porridge because, he claimed, the germ of the oats was so potent that it vanquished the brucella germ in the milk before he had time to swallow it.

His dim imagination was now permanently lodged in the 1930s. He talked of nothing but the Economic War, herding on horseback, the villainies of De Valera, and a long-dead Aberdeen-Angus bull called Henry; and he talked about them with such passion that Kevin often came away wondering if the present-day world of the farm were the real one. His opinions were those of a man who had lost the balancing influence of reason, but Dr. Blizzard said that on no account must they be contradicted. He had had a slight heart attack during the summer, and the doctor told Kevin that he must keep him quiet, that his heart was so weak that it could stop at any moment.

"What's the weather like today?" his father asked as he entered the bedroom.

"It's a fair good day for January," Kevin replied. "Cold but dry. Brass monkey weather for anyone without long johns."

"I'll bet there's shelter in the Grove."

The Grove was a twenty-acre stretch of woodland which his father sold to Murt Quane's father over thirty years ago. He sold it because he was short of money, and the shame of it had eaten so deeply into his heart that he imagined Kevin had bought it back.

"Have you been to the Grove today?" he asked, the thin jaws grinding like those of an old ram chewing the cud.

"No."

"You should walk the Grove every day to let the world know it's ours. People forget. I'm sure there are those who still think it's Quane's. And I hope you're looking after the mare. It's not right to work her with the spavin."

They hadn't had a horse on the farm for twenty years, but that did not matter to his father. Yesterday the mare had angleberries; today she had spavin; tomorrow she'd probably have glanders.

"I'm done enough on this side," his father said. "It's time you turned me over."

He gripped the old man under the arms, but he vehemently shook his birdlike head.

"I've changed my mind. I want to sit up for half an hour."

Kevin got an extra pillow and propped his head against it. The sour breath, like an evening wind blowing over decayed cabbage stumps, struck him like a truncheon in the face.

"My cardigan," his father said, pointing to the foot of the bed.

Kevin helped him on with the threadbare garment and switched off one bar of the electric fire while he wasn't looking. The waste was disgraceful, the electric bills sky high, and mart prices down on last year. He looked at the iron bed, low in the middle like a canoe, which kept his father from falling out. He moved to the foot and felt his father's toes under the clothes, cold like wet clay on newly dug potatoes in November. Slowly, he ran his hand up further to the knee, but his father was too insentient, or perhaps too intent on opening the thermos flask, to notice. He visualized his father in his days of strength, thinning turnips, clawing the brown clay of the drills with both hands. Now the same hands looked as if they had been washed ashore by the tide, seascoured to fragility, with wrinkled skin and branchy veins. His narrow head was too small for his still-wide shoulders, the light skin drawn tightly over jutting bone, accentuating the hollow temples, an egg that threatened to crack and spill its yoke. He turned away with a sense of reeling in his head.

" 'I'll starve John Bull,' said De Valera. 'I'll starve him till he bellows for Irish beef.' And then he promised us a land flowing with milk and honey, but we've drunk little of the milk and tasted less of the honey. A hoor's son in a black overcoat. It's the judgement of the Almighty that he's as blind as a bat," his father called after him.

When he went down to the kitchen, Maureen was mixing the hens' feed. He carved a thin sliver of beef and rubbed it round inside the mustard pot with his forefinger. It was a nuisance having to go all the way to Roscrea for mustard, but there was no alternative—it was, after all, not merely a condiment but a preserver of life.

To give him his due, his passion for mustard had more to do with medicine, as he conceived it, than gastronomy. He saw the first glimmer of light in a Dublin pub after the 1970 All-Ireland hurling final, when an old man who looked pale as death asked him for a pint of stout.

"I'll buy you a pint and welcome if you promise to buy me one back," he replied.

"I'll do better," said the old man. "I'll share with you the secret of longevity, but I'm so parched that I can say no more till you've wet my whistle."

He drank the pint in one gulp and, laying the tumbler on the counter, whispered in Kevin's ear: "Tell it not in Cork, publish it not in the streets of Rosmuck, lest the daughters of Erin rejoice. . . . I am a doctor, an unfrocked doctor, unfrocked by the Minister of Agriculture more than twenty years ago because of my brilliance as a biochemist. In the course of an experiment on the role of *Bacillus cholera suis* in swine fever, I discovered that bacon is carcinogenic. Do you know what that means?" He winked at Kevin.

"No."

"It means that bacon bears the seeds of cancer, and that, my friend, in an agricultural country is political dynamite. You know that ninety per cent of Irish farmers never eat anything for dinner but boiled bacon and cabbage, and if the truth became known the bacon industry would be as good as dead. The Minister of Agriculture, fair play to him, was the first to see it, and he put pressure on the Minister of Health to have my name struck off the register. I was willing to take my case to the highest court, but no counsel would look at me. They all thought I was a raving lunatic. But I promised to tell you my secret. All meat is cancer-bearing except beef, but bacon is the worst offender. The only part of a pig that is free of cancer is the liver, and that you can fry and eat with impunity. But if you take my advice, you will eat no meat, beef included, without the accompaniment of English mustard and a raw onion to kill the bucko. A boiled onion is no good, and neither is French mustard—they're both too mild, you see, to kill the seeds of destruction. And now I'll have another pint if you're buying."

Kevin felt that he was too amusing to deny him a drink, so he bought him a second pint and a third, and all the time they explored in detail the biochemistry of carcinogenic bacon. Convinced at last that his friend was light in the head, Kevin rose to go.

"You may be a bad chemist, but you're a grand talker," he said, shaking hands.

The old man caught his sleeve and winked. "When did you last hear of a rabbi dying of cancer?" he asked fiercely, nodding his head as if he had said the last word on the subject. Kevin soon forgot their conversation, but five years later, soon after the death of his mother, it came back to him when he read in a local paper a letter from a housewife making the same claim for mustard and raw onions as had the "unfrocked" doctor. He had been an eater of boiled bacon all his life, but after reading the letter his thoughts turned to beef. At first he found it flavourless, but like many a late convert he soon repudiated his past tastes with a fervour denied even to his mentor.

"There is something I didn't tell you, Kevin," said Maureen as she sat down at the table.

"What?" he asked when she failed to proceed.

"I'm pregnant."

"You're sure it isn't cloudburst?" He laughed.

"What's that?"

"False pregnancy in goats. The nanny swells up, but

after five months she releases a cloudy liquid and the 'pregnancy' goes away."

"Don't make jokes, Kevin. Coddin' is catchin', and I'm dead worried."

"For God's sake, have a bit of sense. How can you be pregnant now? Haven't we been doing it day in day out for the last three years?"

"I always took care, flushing out your seed when I felt more like sleep. I've no idea how it could've happened. All I know is that I'm a month overdue. Soon I won't be able to go to Mass on Sunday without everyone knowing."

"We'll have to do something about it," he said slowly.

"What can we do?"

"You'll have to go to England till it bursts. I'll send you money every week, and you can come home in two years' time with no one the wiser."

"And what am I to do with the child?"

"Leave it in a home in England if it's a girl, and bring it back with you if it's a boy. You can tell the neighbours that you got married and that your man died in a road accident. If it's a boy, it will be the best thing that's ever happened to us. I won't have to leave the farm and all my tractors to Concepta's little brat, Breffny."

"I'm not going to England with this burden. I've never spent a night away from home, and I've heard terrible things about London. I read in *The Express* only yesterday that one in ten children born there is a bastard."

"All the more reason for going!"

"Don't make fun of me, Kevin. Can't you see I'm troubled?"

"Well, you can't stay here. If you drop a child, the neighbours will know it's mine, because you haven't been seen with any other man. You know what that means, don't you? Incest punishable by imprisonment, not to mention the disgrace."

"The child may not look like you," she pleaded.

She looked haggard and unfriended, lines of worry showing round her kindly eyes and mouth. He wanted to comfort her, but he still could not believe her.

"You mean I'm not a colour-marking breed?" he asked.

"What are you talking about?"

"If you take a cow to a Hereford bull, her calf will have a white face; and if you take her to an Aberdeen-Angus, her calf will be born black. A Shorthorn bull, on the other hand, leaves no definite colour mark. Are you saying that I may be a Shorthorn?"

"There's no good talking to you in this mood."

"It's a pity we've been born before our time. In a few hundred years incest will be as common as ditch water and as dull too. You see, when they first started inbreeding cattle, the Holy Marys said it was incest, that it was against God's law. But the farmers won the argument. They said that they were breeding the best to the best, a good bull to his sister or even to his mother."

"Why do you have to bring farming into everything?" she moaned.

She put both hands to her face, and he could see from the shaking of her shoulders that she was sobbing. Awkwardly, he crossed the floor and put his hand on her arm.

"Don't cry, Maureen. Sure, I was only making fun. Leave it to me. I'm sure to find a way."

She went upstairs, drying her eyes. He slumped into her chair and stared at the nearest hedge through the curtainless window. The afternoon had darkened. The forbidding sky looked as if it were about to descend with the night and press men and cattle into the ground. His mind moved slowly over a dim tract of land, hovered for a moment before swooping on a field. His winter barley, sown in late September, was doing well; with luck it would be better than last year, when the yield was three tonnes to the acre at seventeen per cent moisture. The trick was to sow early and allow for good plant establishment. Murt Quane, who sowed in early December, had a yield of less than two tonnes, and to get that he had to sow twelve stone to the acre as opposed to Kevin's nine. He would have to keep an eye on his cattle, though. One of his spring-calving cows was thin. He had dried her off before the others and he was feeding her to appetite, but still she wasn't responding. Perhaps a word with Festus O'Flaherty tomorrow evening would do the trick.

Slowly, he rephrased the question on his mind. The real problem was not one of unwanted pregnancy but that of finding an acceptable "father" to satisfy the hypocritical convention that a woman must not give birth unless she has known a man who is not her brother. Sadly, the only men who came to Clonglass were the parish priest and the postman. The parish priest was a seventy-five-year-old misogynist who had long since slapped down his final erection; and the postman, a landless bachelor, took the post so seriously that he saw the world, women included, merely as writers and recipients of letters. He would have to find another man, a younger man, a rambling, roving man who scattered his seed along the highways and byways with ne'er a thought for the sprouting. If she were to know such a man, she could fill the house with children for all he cared. But, come to think of it, one was enough—provided it was a boy.

2

Getting up from the chair, he stretched himself and went outside, still aware of the dull ache in his testicles. Henry was in the bull yard, a faraway look in his ox eye. By long tradition the stock bull at Clonglass was called Henry in commemoration of the sexual vigour of Henry VIII, and by an equally venerable tradition the bull on the nearest Protestant farm was called Alex in honour of Pope Alexander VI, who, according to O'Flaherty, knew as much about incest as incense. The present Henry was old, heavy, ill-tempered, and truculent. At night he lived in a loose box attached to which was the bull yard and service pen. He was a good bull in spite of his vicious temper, a trifle hard on young heifers perhaps and not as gentlemanly as the previous Henry, but the soul of sexual efficiency, nonetheless. After one sniff of a cow in heat, he would come on form at once, and Kevin and Maureen liked nothing better than watching him in service, giving the full power of his hindquarters to each drive, his bulbous eyes staring straight in front of him, the folds of his dewlap resting on the cow's back, his fierce breath warming her wilting withers.

Life was not all pleasure for Henry, however. Tethered alone in a field in summer, he would raise his head and bellow for beautiful heifers denied him by his chain; and on one occasion Kevin found him masturbating sadly against a post. He had never felt a stronger sense of kinship with Henry than he did then, and if he'd had a pretty heifer in heat he would have led her to him on the spot.

Kevin now rested his elbows on the wall of the bull yard, wondering if Henry had ever experienced testicular pain after service. Then a shaft of thought lit up his face. He was meeting Festus O'Flaherty, the local vet, tomorrow evening, and he would tell him that Henry seemed to have a pain in the scrotum, just to see what he might say. He could not really go to Dr. Blizzard, in case the pain was connected with sex. Blizzard, like everyone else in the parish, knew that he did not go out with women; and if the pain was one that no good-living Catholic should have, the good doctor might put two and two together.

Kevin always went to Killage on Saturday evenings. First he would make the round of the shops that were open late, picking up a few necessaries such as mustard and any odds and ends he felt reluctant to entrust to a woman—shaving lather, razor blades, pipe tobacco, and three bottles of whiskey to see his father through the week. After the shopping he would go to Phelan's Hotel to meet Festus O'Flaherty, a Connemara man who had made his home in the midlands. The midland farmers liked him in spite of his accent. They said that he was a good vet, that he called a beast a "baste," that he took sick cattle more seriously than Dr. Blizzard took his patients; and in turn O'Flaherty had nothing but praise for the farmers he served. He said that they regarded a vet's fee as a debt of honour, that they cared for their cattle even better than they cared for their wives, and that, because of the vet's position in rural society, they liked nothing better than buying him drinks. He occasionally even praised them for their philosophy. "Unlike Connemara men," he would say, "midlanders take themselves seriously. When they laugh, they know it."

Kevin liked O'Flaherty too. He first met him in a pub after a ploughing match, and since then they had taken to meeting every Saturday evening at Phelan's. At first they talked about cattle, but as their friendship grew they talked less about cows and more about women. Though O'Flaherty was married, he had not lost his sense of romance. He still fell in love easily, but never for more than a night at a time. Kevin had already decided to invite him to have a look at Henry, and now it occurred to him that after the diagnosis he would invite him into the house to meet Maureen. As a ladies' man, he was a good candidate for the job. If he took a fancy to her, he would lay her quickly and cleanly and then leave her. It was a measure of Kevin's affection for him that O'Flaherty was one of the few men he could calmly contemplate in a clinch with Maureen.

All day on Saturday, as he wished for the evening, he was aware of his carnal knowledge of his sister like a submerged rock inside his head. Like a rock, his knowledge of her had mass or inertia. It resisted his every effort to move or dislodge it. It was there as Slieve Bloom was there or the land which he ploughed and harrowed. While talking to Maureen, he always concealed the seriousness with which he regarded their relationship, but alone in the cab of a tractor he had no choice but to confront his conscience, which told him that incest was wrong. The state said that it was a crime punishable by imprisonment, and the priests said that it was a sin punishable by spiritual death. It was the imprisonment that worried him most, however. The wages of sin might be death, but death was always tomorrow. For the hundredth time he wondered if the incest taboo was God-given or man-made. In the Book of Genesis, Lot slept with his daughters and God blessed their union with two sons. And if the story of Adam and Eve were true, it followed that we are all children of incest. But though it might be a sin to puncture your sister's maidenhead, it was not the worst sin in the book. It was not as bad as buggery, for example, which must surely be very unhygienic. And it wasn't as bad as bestiality.

He put the tractor into reverse and paused to wonder if he had judged correctly. The priests claimed that in sexual sin with another person the possibility of scandal was always present. They would lean over the pulpit and thunder, "Woe unto the scandal-giver. . . . It were better for him that a mill-stone were hanged about his neck and he cast into the sea." Now, the great thing about bestiality was that you could not give scandal to a beast, and therefore you might be led to think that the Pope would count it a less dangerous sin than incest. But, though no priest had told him so, he suspected that bestiality with an attractive Hereford heifer would be a bigger sin than incest with a flat-footed sister, not because the young heifer might be more beautiful than the sister but because the human body was, as Paul had told the Corinthians, "the temple of the Holy Ghost." Therefore, to copulate with a brute beast was to commit the ultimate sin in human degradation. That was something for which he was thankful. At least Maureen was not a Hereford.

He left the field at one and spent the afternoon doing odd jobs about the yard until it was time to feed the animals. Usually, he did not go to Phelan's till after nine, but tonight he would go at eight and have a few pints alone before O'Flaherty arrived. After tea he washed and shaved, put on his good suit, polished his Sunday shoes with an old pair of Maureen's knickers. At last it was time to go. His Mercedes was slow to start, so he fiddled with the choke for a moment before turning the ignition key again. He was proud of his Mercedes, which he had bought last autumn after selling his fatted calves. At first he felt self-conscious behind the big wheel, recalling the old Morris he'd had for eleven years, but soon he got accustomed to the extra width and length; and when other farmers made jokes about the amount of petrol it consumed, he would pretend he had not heard and merely say, "They're handy yokes." He did not drive it very often, only on mart days, on Sunday mornings to go to Mass, and on Saturday evenings going to Killage. At first he had wondered if it might be too flashy for a farmer who more often than not would have a trailer on tow, but he soon solved that problem by omitting to clean it. After a month or so the wings and doors were splashed by cow dung and farmyard slurry, and then he felt as much at home in it as if he'd been conceived and born on the back seat.

Festus O'Flaherty was in the cocktail bar forcing drink on a fat farmer who was obviously eager to go home.

"Do you know the first commandment in extramarital sex?" Festus asked him.

"Thou shalt not covet thy neighbour's wife," said the farmer, trying to release the vet's vicious grip on his arm.

"No, no," shouted Festus. "The first commandment in extramarital sex is 'Thou shalt not shit on thine own doorstep.'"

"Believe me, I believe you," said the farmer.

"And do you know the second?"

"Let me go home to my wife like a good man."

"Do you know the second law of extramarital sex?" Festus repeated.

"No."

"It is impossible to produce an erection by transferring heat from a cold body to a hot body in any self-sustaining process. Ah, Kevin, me darling, me onlie begetter of foggage and its myriad applications!"

Festus put an arm round Kevin's neck, and the fat farmer seized the heaven-sent opportunity to escape.

"Kevin, you're early, but not a minute too soon. I was telling this bugger from Borris—where's he gone?—about extramarital sex, and all he could think of was how soon he could get home to his wife. I even told him the second law of thermodynamics, suitably edited of course, and he still failed to get even the teeniest erection."

"You're drunk three hours ahead of schedule," said Kevin.

"If I'm drunk, it's not without reason. I was called out to Lackey this evening to look at a sick cow, but it was too late. Too far gone. Some men are donkeys."

"You take life too seriously."

"But not life in the sense you mean it."

They took their drinks to a table in the corner and sat down. Phelan's cocktail bar was new. It was the only cocktail bar in Killage, a market town with a population of 1,000 which boasted thirty pubs, one supermarket, two news-agents, and two petrol filling stations. The cocktail bar was patronized mainly by bank employees, shopkeepers, businessmen, and well-to-do farmers with wives who would not be seen dead in a mere pub. For this reason it had an air of unreality which acted synergistically on patrons who came in to forget the outside world. The low glass-topped tables, the red plush seats, and the dim lights concealed cunningly in the ceiling made Kevin wonder why he came. To that there was only one answer: He came because O'Flaherty came. When it first opened, the landlord decreed that it was first and foremost a doubles bar, that those who drank stout must drink it like ladies, from half-pink glasses with delicate stems; and when his patrons responded by ordering two glasses each time instead of one, he was sufficiently good-humoured to realize that he was on a loser, that the social aspirations of bank managers' wives were unlikely to change the drinking habits of a man-dominated community that derived its philosophy from the vagaries of the weather and its income from tillage and cattle.

"Have you ever heard of a bull with a pain in his balls?" Kevin asked after the first pint.

"I've been up to my right armpit in cattle all day. For God's sake have mercy on me, will you, in the evening. But I must tell you, I must tell you about the nicest thing that's happened to me this week. I went over to Craigstown on Monday to have a look at a bull with strangury, and while I was there I met a well-preserved widow from Clonaslew who invited me to a whist drive the following evening. Now, as you know, I detest whist and all games of chance except the extramarital, but because she had weathered so well I accepted her invitation. It was lucky I did, because as soon as the last card was played she invited me back for a nightcap, which led to a conversation, which led to a kiss, which led to a slap, which led to an intercrural tickle."

"Did she laugh to show she had some tickles left?"

"No, she was more original. She asked me if it were possible for a woman to hatch a hen egg in the heat of her oxter."

"And what did you say?"

"I told her that I would go away and think about it. I said it because I could not think of a witty answer, but as it happened it was the best answer, because it gave her an excuse to ring me. To cut a long story short, she invited me to dinner. She gave me leek soup, grilled trout, veal and ham, which she swore was saltimbocca, stuffed peaches, and brandy and port that made me so randy that I couldn't climb the stairs. It was not an irreparable tragedy, however, because she had a tiger skin in front of the log fire that was softer than any featherbed. The real tragedy is that now as I look back I cannot remember her face. All I can recall is the jangling of her bangles as I came, which reminded me of the sleighbells in Mahler's Fourth Symphony."

"I've been meaning to ask you about Henry," Kevin said in despair.

"You know, there are times when I think you don't come here for the brilliance of my conversation but for the benefit of my veterinary advice. Don't rush me, Kevin. Henry is now in his loose box, dreaming of Friesians, which to him are more beautiful than any woman either of us is likely to meet. Have you ever thought of that? Of the high standard of beauty among heifers? You may laugh, but I'm serious. Just ask yourself when you last saw an ugly heifer, and then ask yourself when you last saw an ugly woman."

O'Flaherty's thumb was biting into Kevin's biceps, but Kevin, pretending not to be in pain, took another slug from his tumbler. O'Flaherty was tipsy, and his tipsiness was accentuated by the shock of red hair that kept falling down over his left eye. He was a big man with a fresh complexion and a ready smile that gave his face the look of a precocious baby's. Kevin often wondered about him, about the softness of his features and his lack of manly stubble. It was odd that such a man should come from a wasteland of granite and quartzite like Connemara, and it was strange that in spite of the diversity of his sexual experience he should still bear in his countenance the marks of innocence. It was as if life had not touched him, which might well account for his success with widows and faithless wives. They all thought that he was lea land, but in this they were wrong. O'Flaherty was a jester, a laughing carefree man whose first allegiance was to cattle. He loved cattle. He talked to them as he treated them, and he remembered with unerring accuracy their case histories and the case histories of their progenitors. He was in every respect a professional, a quality that never showed to greater effect than when he was called out early on a Monday morning with a scalp-raising hangover. On one such morning Kevin saw him cast a cranky Aberdeen-Angus bull with an effortless expertise he would never forget, the kind of art and scope he himself would love to possess. It was such a pity that O'Flaherty had a heart of stone.

"I've thought of nothing but the widow for the last three days." Festus sighed.

"Do I know her?" Kevin asked.

"She's Rita Heaviside. She has a big house this side of Clonaslew and two bay hunters in the stable. For a woman who rides she has the smallest bottom you've ever seen, like two bantam eggs in a pocket handkerchief, so neat that I can span it like that with one hand. It even makes me want to break the third commandment of extramarital sex, the one that says thou shalt not commit adultery twice with the same woman. To be honest, I wouldn't mind giving her a good rumbling, what I call a cockamaroo, this very minute. It's very possible that I'm falling in love with her."

This was bad news. O'Flaherty normally looked at women with a cold, unblinking eye that never looked twice in the same direction. It was one of his axioms that the adulteress had not been born who could tempt him to an encore. If he was going to fall in love with the widow Heaviside, how could he interest him in Maureen?

"Ah, she's only a passing fancy," Kevin said. "A man will often fall in love with a woman for two or three days and then forget her. It's a natural enough reaction to cold weather."

"Have you ever been in love?"

"Once with a woman I never as much as spoke to. I just saw her on a train and she accidentally touched my knee."

27

"Tell me about her," said Festus.

Kevin told the story of the girl in the off-white bra while Festus pulled on his cigar and nodded.

"She wasn't a real girl," he said when Kevin had ended. "She's a fantasy girl. Nearly every man has one of those in his life, especially men who have fallen in love with themselves."

"Have you got one?"

"Mine is a train girl too, but she's different from yours. She appeared to me on the Galway–Dublin train about four years ago. She got on at Athenry and we found ourselves alone, sitting opposite each other with neither book nor newspaper. She didn't say a word, just opened her legs and closed them quickly again, as if she were flashing messages at sea. At first I was too shy to look, but then I told myself to treat it like a free magic lantern show. She kept opening and closing her legs, and all the time she was leaving them open for a fraction of a second longer. Then I saw it, a big pink sea shell with a mouth full of folds, set in reddish seaweed. At first I was horrified by the grossness of it, and then I realized that what I had seen was a surrealist picture painted by a pointillist on her panties. I knew because the hair on her "fanny" was red while the hair on her head was a lustrous black. I looked up at the ceiling and laughed, and she flashed again but not long enough for me to read the signature on the painting. Now, she is *my* train girl," said O'Flaherty.

Kevin felt ashamed for having given O'Flaherty such an opportunity. He had taken his precious girl in the off-white bra and turned her into a trollop. You should never talk seriously about sex with other men, he told himself. They never tell the truth, they just stamp on your dreams.

"You haven't answered my question about Henry," Kevin said.

"What about Henry?"

"He's standing on one hind leg, rubbing the inside of the other against his balls as if he were in pain. Can a bull have a pain in his briefcase?"

"I suppose he can, just as you or I can."

"What could it be?"

"Any one of a number of ailments. It could be epididymitis, for example, but I'd have to examine him to know."

"And what's epididymitis?"

"Inflammation of the epididymis, which is attached to the testicles. I had better have a look at him right away."

"Is there such a thing as cancer down there?"

"I've never come across a case in a bull, but I had a friend at university who got cancer of the scrotum at twenty-one, poor devil."

"Did he die?" Kevin tried to sound casual.

"He spent a while on radiation treatment and he lost so much weight that he became a shadow of his former self."

"Did he die?" Kevin repeated.

"Oh, yes, he died all right. What horrified me most, however, was not his death but the callousness of the doctor who said that he snuffed it trying to sing the *Nunc dimittis* in soprano."

Festus had passed across the march between tipsiness and drunkenness. He had to make two attempts on the phrase *Nunc dimittis,* his eyelids kept closing, and he spoke with a cigar in one corner of his mouth and the words in the other. At any moment now he would get up from the table and walk round the bar offering to buy a drink for anyone who could define the categorical imperative. Everyone who came into Phelan's had heard the phrase at least once a week, but so far no one had managed to construe it.

"It's time you issued your weekly challenge," Kevin said.

"Not tonight. I'm going home with you now to look at Henry."

"Henry is fast asleep. His briefcase can wait till tomorrow."

"You hard-hearted bugger," said O'Flaherty, gripping Kevin's left knee. "How would you like to have a pain in your ballocks?"

They left the bar, Kevin wondering how he could persuade Festus to go straight home. If he came to Clonglass now, Maureen would be in bed and the visit would not achieve its intended purpose. Outside, Festus found that luck was against him. First, he could not find his car, and then, having found it, he discovered to his amazement that the ignition key was too big for the keyhole.

"Come on, Festus, you're not fit to drive. Leave your car here and collect it in the morning. Jump in with me and I'll drive you home."

"But I'm going to see Henry. An animal in pain is an animal in need of me."

"Look, Festus, there's no electric light in the loose box. More than likely, you'll have to cast the bastard, and how can you cast a bad-tempered bull in the dark?"

"There's no justice in the world. Here we are, enjoying the fleshpots of Killage while Henry writhes in agony in his loose box."

After much pleading and coaxing, Kevin bundled him into the Mercedes and drove the short distance down the road to his house. O'Flaherty pressed him to come in for a drink, but Kevin had no ambition to be used as a decoy in the nightly skirmish between Festus and his wife. She detested drunkenness, and for reasons of his own Festus contrived to give her the impression that he was drunk more often than he was. He would come home, singing his head off in Irish, at three o'clock in the morning for the simple reason that he did not want her to know that he had spent the previous three hours in another woman's bed. And as she was convinced that he was a man of only one vice, she stayed with him in the hope of eventual reformation. Though their battles were legendary, and though she had crowned him with a skillet more than once, Festus respected her and needed her too. It seemed to Kevin that his third commandment, which forbade the committing of adultery twice with the same woman, had been formulated expressly to ensure that his wife would have less chance of finding him out.

Kevin drove home alone. The road ran straight, gently undulating between leafless hedges, and he drove carefully, stopping at each blind crossroads, because he knew that he was slightly drunk. As the car came through the gate, Pup came round the corner of the hay shed furiously wagging his tail. Kevin got out, gave him a kick in the side, and shivered because the night was cold. As he stood in the lee of the hay shed waiting for his water to come, a fox barked sharply in the Grove. He felt defeated by the night. The pain had left his testicles, but he was still aware of it as he was aware of the emptiness of the landscape. He remembered once dosing a calf with poteen on Christmas morning, and the memory warmed him as the poteen had warmed the calf. Neverthe-less, the past seemed such a long stretch of faceless time. He wondered if the future, when it had been strained through the present into the past, would seem so featureless, and he was grateful that he did not know. The fox barked again, and as he cocked his ear he drew comfort from the gentle breath-ing of the cattle in the cow houses.

He took off his shoes and sat in front of the range in the kitchen wiggling his toes, waiting for the kettle to boil. He had felt constrained in Phelan's because he could not be straight with Festus. He was a man of secrets, or at least one secret that was so heavy that it felt like a turnip in the pit of his stomach. If only he could go down to the Grove and whisper it to one of the larches for relief. But there was no relief. Life itself was wrapped in secrecy. The great arches of life—birth, copulation, death—were the things that people most often concealed. When Concepta was born, he and Maureen played in the kitchen while the midwife was busy in the bedroom. They did not know that she was a midwife. All they had been told was that their mother was too unwell to make their tea, and that the midwife had come to look after them. And when his mother lay dying of cancer, their father decreed that she must not be told the name of the dread disease. She must be made to think that she was recovering from a successful operation for gallstones, that she would be up and about in six weeks. The terrible pain would go away and all would be well again. She lay in the canoelike bed, not eating, not speaking, until one day she called for Kevin.

"Kevin," she said. "You were always a sensible lad. What's wrong with me?"

"Nothing," he said. "The gallstones have been removed and you'll be better before you know."

"Kevin, you're a man now. You don't have to sniff your father's heels."

Ashamed, he went downstairs and out into the field to thin fodder beet, but all day he could only think of her face. He came in at nightfall and went straight to her room. She was lying on her back, the sheet tucked under the unflinching chin, her dark eyes closed. He was reluctant to wake her, and he turned to the door.

"What did you come to say to me, Kevin?" she asked without opening her eyes.

"You have cancer, Mother, cancer of the stomach, and I'm sorry. The gallstones were Daddy's idea. He didn't want you to worry."

She opened her eyes and offered him a thin hand. It was

the first time she had touched him voluntarily since he was a boy.

"I can face the devil I know," she said, closing her eyes again.

He stood in the dark bedroom uneasily holding her hand until she inquired if Maureen had found the nest of the bantam that had been laying out.

He went down the stairs questioning the emptiness in his mind. He went out into the twilight, hopped on his tractor, and had reached the gate before he knew what he was doing.

"Life is loss, life is loss, life is loss," he repeated aloud. The words seemed to come from nowhere, as if someone else had put them in his mouth, as if there had been no corresponding thought in his mind.

He was up at eight the following morning, in time to see the paling of the sky behind the Grove. As soon as he came down, he took the big kettle from the range and put it over a low gas so that it would have boiled by the time he had done his jobs. No sooner had he foddered the animals and sat down to his breakfast of cold beef and mustard than he heard the purr of a car in the yard. It was Festus in a donkey jacket, flushed and wind-swept, inquiring after the state of Henry's health. Kevin told him that Henry was much improved, that he had stopped chafing his briefcase with his hind leg, that there was really no need to worry. Festus, however, had other ideas.

"It may be one of those symptoms that come and go. Now that I'm here I'm going to get to the root of it."

As if in reply to his expressed intention, there was a rattling of chains in the loose box and Henry emerged into the bull yard. Festus expanded his chest and with arm outstretched declaimed:

"O piebald king, great-pintled aurochs!
    Are you the cock, the scrotum or the ballocks?"

He entered the bull yard and walked round Henry with his
hands in the pockets of his donkey jacket.

"He doesn't look like an animal in pain, but his hooves
could do with a trim. I'm surprised you've allowed them to
grow so long. Come on, we'll cast him first, and after I've
felt the contents of his briefcase I might even do a manicuring
job on his feet for you."

"I think you're wasting your time, Festus. He's better.
You can tell from the way he's standing. Yesterday he was
standing with a hump as if he couldn't bear the cold."

"Is there a dry field where we can cast him? It will only
take fifteen minutes."

By now Kevin had realized that Festus would not leave
till he'd made a thorough examination of Henry's testi-
monials, so he went into the house and told Maureen to put
on her finery, that he would ask Festus in for a drink as soon
as they had dealt with Henry.

He got ropes from the shed and handed them to Festus.
Then he put a mask over Henry's eyes and, with the aid of a
bull staff hooked to his nose ring, led him out to the nearest
field. They cast Henry without too much trouble, and when
he was lying on his side Festus touched his scrotum with his
hand. At first Henry tried to kick with one of his hind legs,
but the ropes held him prisoner. Then, as if he had suddenly
changed his mind, he lay still, breathing heavily against the
hard ground.

"There's nothing the matter with Henry. He's beginning
to enjoy it," said Festus, noting the bull's enviably healthy
erection.

"It's interesting that a bull's, though it lengthens, doesn't
thicken as much as a stallion's," said Kevin.

"Yes, a bull has a lower coefficient of expansion."

"In that case a man is more like a stallion."

"Do you think I should give him a helping hand out of his misery?" Festus asked, caressing the great penis with his fingertips.

"It's an odd thing to do on Sunday morning, and neither of us has yet been to Mass."

Henry groaned with enjoyment as Festus continued to stroke him. Kevin moved sideways out of the firing line, but there really was no need, because whatever Henry had been suffering from it was not *ejaculatio praecox*.

"He's a true gentleman," said Festus, beginning to recognize the impossibility of the task he'd set himself.

"He knows the difference between oats and onions."

"He knows the difference between the temperature of a man's hand and of a cow's vulva."

"Will you come in for a hair of the dog before you go?" Kevin asked when they had led Henry back to the yard.

"I can only stay a minute. I promised to meet the widow for a quick drink and a twankydillo after late Mass in Clonaslew."

Kevin poured large whiskeys and put plenty of water in his own because he was not a spirits drinker.

"Take off your coat and sit down," he said, wondering what could be keeping Maureen.

"Do you really think it's a sin to wank a bull?" Festus laughed.

"I suppose it would depend on whether you got pleasure from it."

"You don't think I need confess it, then?"

"Not unless it troubles you."

"There are worse sins in the book than wanking bulls."

"Buggery and bestiality," suggested Kevin.

"There's worse than that."

Kevin looked at him, wondering if he were going to say incest. He waited for a moment, but Festus seemed to have lost the thread of his thought.

"What is the worst sexual sin, then?" Kevin asked.

"*Congressus cum Daemone,* intercourse with the devil."

Kevin gave a roar of a laugh, but Festus stared at him as if he were too witless to recognize truth when he heard it.

A clomping on the stairs warned Kevin that Maureen had finished her toilet. She appeared at the door in ladderless stockings, high heels, and a black taffeta skirt with big red flowers above the hem. And as if that were not enough, she had put red war paint on her cheeks. She looked across at Festus like a gypsy at a horse fair about to ask a man to cross her hand with silver.

"You know Maureen?" Kevin said.

Festus took her hand, and she vanished into the parlour as if she had suddenly taken fright at his touch. After two or three minutes she came out again with a plate of sweet biscuits and offered him one.

"No, thanks, I don't eat sweet things when I'm drinking," he said kindly, but Kevin could see that he thought her odd.

"I'll make you a cup of tea to have with the biscuits, then," she said.

"No, thanks just the same. I must be leaving in a minute."

"Have another hair of another dog," Kevin said in an attempt to keep the party going.

He poured Festus another whiskey, and they both talked about mart prices while Maureen sat at the table, loudly munching the sweet biscuits. After a while Festus rose to go. Kevin went out to see him off, and when he came back

Maureen ran to him sobbing. He held her unwillingly, annoyed because she had embarrassed him in front of Festus.

"He never once looked at me," she kept saying through her tears. "And after me putting on all my best things."

"Pull yourself together," he said at last. "If you don't dally, we'll make late Mass in Killage."

3

Kevin was not a man who accepted one season and rejected another. He loved luxuriant summer, but he loved naked winter too, because in the course of the year there was a time for every purpose under heaven . . . a time to plant, and a time to pluck up that which is planted . . . a time to break down and a time to build up. As he looked round the bare hedges and faded fields poached black in gateways, he recalled his old winter pleasure of stall-feeding cattle in the short days, and he realized that now his pleasure had receded, that when he pulped fodder beet and rolled oats and put them in buckets, his mind ran implacably in a slurry gripe from which there was no escape. He knew that there was a time to keep silence, but he wondered if there was a time to speak. Between him and other men, even Festus O'Flaherty and Murt Quane, there was empty reticence. When they looked at him, they saw the shell of the man they had known for years, but they did not see the man he had become. He was the custodian of a secret which set him apart from his friends, a cancerous secret that by a process of metastasis drew all strength and purpose from his thoughts.

At times he would say to himself that he was like any other man, that many an Irish countryman had known his sister's flesh, that he himself differed from the others only in knowing what was forbidden over a longer period. He wasn't different; he was merely worse. Was it now too late to escape the fury that had probably already been unleashed? The pain in his testicles had worried him, but for the past few days he had been free of it. Was that because he had not touched Maureen since she told him that she was pregnant? Was there, in other words, a means by which he could recover his former self? Or must he sit under the heavens like a rock in an open field waiting for the bolt of lightning that will split it?

Huddled in the tractor cab as he spread brown slurry on hard ground, he asked himself what form his punishment would take. Sickness—a gripe in the bowels followed by a slow and terrifying death like his mother's, an end of screaming and praying for release? A seemingly meaningless accident—a windy day and a beech tree falling on him in the lane? Blighted crops or foot and mouth disease among the herd? He recalled the Capuchin missionary raising the roof of Killage chapel with fearful thunder:

"Be not deceived; God is not mocked; for whatever a man soweth, that shall he also reap. . . . For I the Lord thy God am a jealous God and visit the sins of the fathers upon the children unto the third and fourth generation."

Did the same jealous God visit the still uncommitted sins of the sons on the mothers as well? He wished that he could settle once and for all the only theological question that ever plagued him—Did God make Man or did Man make God? It was a question which each man must answer for himself, a question on which the opinion of a fool was as good as the opinion of a philosopher. He thought of his life, and knew that though he might flirt with the idea of a godless universe his nature must ultimately reject it. He was a prisoner of time, of place, of the singleness of his own experience.

At dinnertime Maureen told him that she was going to write to Concepta. "I must confide in someone or I'll go mad," she said.

"Well, don't invite her here. I can stand her even less than I can stand her ass of a husband."

"But she said in her letter that she was coming anyhow."

"I don't want you to tell her anything."

"What will I do, then?"

"I'll find another man for you."

"Who?"

"I don't know yet."

"What about Murt Quane?" she asked without looking at him.

He peeled four potatoes, dipped his knife in the mustard, and spread a thin lick of it over the lean beef. Maureen never mashed swedes. She always served them in thick slices, so he mashed both swede and potato together with his fork, savouring the sweetness of the steam that rose into his face. Maureen's spoon rattled in her soup mug, but still he was silent, because Murt Quane was his best friend, closer to him than Festus O'Flaherty. Murt and he helped each other whenever farm work required cooperation, they lent each other machinery, and in winter Kevin often went to Quane's to ramble. Murt was five years younger than Kevin, and like Kevin he was big-boned and handsome in a rough-cast way; but more important he shared with Kevin a dry sense of humour that enabled them both to talk seriously while knowing that their conversation was leading inevitably to a burst of raillery and the release of glorious laughter.

Perhaps another reason why they enjoyed each other's company was that neither of them was encumbered by a close relationship with a woman outside the family. Like Kevin, Murt lived with his sister, but she was a sister, Kevin knew, who had not taught him the way to her bed. He had a girl friend in Roscrea, a farmer's daughter with a degree in agriculture, whom he met on Sunday evenings, but, as he never mentioned her, Kevin assumed that he sought her company merely for her agricultural conversation. Kevin had once seen her picture in *The Farmers' Journal*. It had been taken at an IFA dinner dance, and from it he could see that her greatest asset as a woman was her Bachelor of Agricultural Science degree. This discovery did not displease him, because he himself did not mind being a bachelor as long as he had the eligible Murt Quane for company. For reasons of his own, Murt seldom came to Clonglass to ramble, and Kevin felt that to invite him now might seem strange. Besides, their friendship was precious, too precious to jeopardize, even to get Maureen out of a quandary.

"He's the right age," said Maureen, sucking the last of the barley from the bottom of her mug.

"He's got a woman already."

"Who?"

"A girl called Polly Nangle from Roscrea."

"You could ask him up this afternoon to help you with the shed."

He broke a rib off the joint, and holding it in his left hand, he began tearing the meat from it with his knife. When he had finished, he chewed the soft end of the bone and then sucked it like a man prospecting for marrow.

Aware of Maureen's gaze, he thought that her idea might be turned to advantage. The shed was ready for roofing, and for main rafters he had bought secondhand iron girders which were too heavy for one man to handle. He could ask Murt to give him a helping hand and at the same time placate Maureen while he was thinking of a more practical solution. Of one thing he was certain: he would not involve his friend in anything that he would not wish upon himself.

"I was thinking of asking him to help with the girders next week, but since the day is dry I'll go down to Larch Lawn to see if he can come this afternoon."

"He could have his tea here," she said enthusiastically. "I've got ham and tomatoes and a sponge cake I bought in case Concepta decided to surprise us."

It was two o'clock when he swung into Quane's immaculate farmyard. He was surprised to see Murt's sister, Elizabeth, coming out of the garden. She taught in a primary school in Killage, and he expected her to be still at work.

"It's well for some." He smiled. "Five half-days and the week is over."

"We deserved our break today. We had the inspector in this morning and then the manager, who said that we could close early."

He seldom spoke to Elizabeth alone, and now he looked over his shoulder as if he expected Murt to come to his assistance. She always made fun of himself and Murt, pretending that she knew nothing of farming, that their very conversation was Greek to her. She looked at the aluminum basin in her hand, waiting for him to declare his business.

"Have you seen Murt?" he asked, hoping that her reply would not be too complicated.

"I think I saw him go into the dairy five minutes ago. If you have a look round, you're bound to find him."

"I'll be seeing you," he said with a little smile, glad to get away.

He found Murt in the pulper house pulping turnips, and he leant for a moment against the doorjamb listening to the hum of the electric motor before he spoke.

"I've just seen her," he said.

"And what do you think?" Murt switched off the pulper.

"She's lovely."

"Would you like to try her out?"

"I wouldn't mind."

They both returned to the yard and walked admiringly round Murt's new tractor.

"It's the roomiest cab you've ever seen," said Murt, handing him the key.

Kevin jumped in and started the engine, eased forward, reversed, and did a complete turn.

"She's quiet for a heavy tractor. You won't need ear-plugs, and that's a fact."

"She's got one fault and it's serious. The PTO shaft keeps revolving even when the lever is in neutral. I'm taking her back to the garage to ask them to fix it."

"Will you be selling the old one?"

"No, I'll keep her for light work."

"Are you two still talking about foggage?" Elizabeth laughed as she joined them.

"I only talk about foggage in the autumn, but Kevin talks about it all the year round. He's giving a lecture about it to the Mountmellick Macra next Sunday."

"Do you want to come?" Kevin smiled at her. Now that Murt was here, he felt that he could relax in her company. She wasn't as pretty as Murt was handsome, but she was clean of limb, straight in the back, and light on her little feet.

"If you want to know about foggage, Kevin's your man," Murt said.

"What were you talking about then?" she asked.

"Timothy," Kevin laughed.

"Timothy who?"

"Not the friend of St. Paul but the companion of cocks-foot and fescue."

"Ah, a species of grass. I'm not as innocent as I look." She smiled.

"Kevin is coddin' you," said Murt. "We were discussing PTO."

"Please turn over?"

"The power take-off shaft of the tractor, that little rod at the back that keeps revolving so that you can work anything off it, from a mower to a cement mixer."

"You're like two schoolboys with a new toy. You won't be happy till you've broken it."

They both watched her disappear into the house, and as they talked, they could hear her piano music flowing like coloured streamers through the open window.

"I'll be up in half an hour," said Murt as Kevin got into the Mercedes.

He drove down the tree-sheltered lane, remembering it in summer when the rich foliage made a dark-green arch that kept out the sky. Yet darkness was not a quality that he associated with Larch Lawn. It was an airy, well-ordered place, and Murt's and Elizabeth's badinage gave it an echo of laughter. The house was new, built by their late father less than ten years ago, and it looked as if it were situated in open parkland, as if it were not a farmer's home at all. Clonglass on the other hand hunkered behind a defensive line of trees. The house was old, stone-built and slate-roofed, and the trees to the north darkened the kitchen on the brightest day of summer. It would be wrong to say, however, that Clonglass was dark and Larch Lawn light; more true to say that Clonglass was silent and secretive and Larch Lawn open-hearted, a place the world could see from the road without wondering what went on inside.

Murt and Elizabeth, though only five years younger, behaved as if they belonged to a different generation from Maureen and himself. They were brighter, more confident, with greater expectations from everyday living, and Elizabeth brought the world at large into the house, talking knowledgeably about television and the newspapers, illuminating each topic with the glint of her personality, whereas Maureen talked mainly of hens and the farmyard. Perhaps they differed because of their different upbringings. Kevin's father was a stern, tight-fisted man who, in spite of his worldly talk, had failed in everything he turned his hand to, whereas Murt's father was a jolly, companionable sort who always went for a drink on market day and after Mass on Sunday. With neither huffing nor puffing, he doubled the acreage of his farm, while Kevin's father was forced by bad management to sell a fifth of his, including the never-to-be-forgotten Grove. Since taking over the farm from his father, Kevin had more than recovered the lost ground, but he had not recovered what little respect he once had for the old man. He was a shadow that could not be penetrated by light, a putrefying afterbirth that could not be shed. All he was good for was lambasting Dev, wasting electricity, and pouring whiskey down his withered gullet. He never swallowed whiskey when he had to pay for it out of his own pocket.

Kevin did not want to think about his father, so he visualized the black ribbon in Elizabeth's hair which matched her black blouse which went well with her tight white skirt. There was nothing more attractive than a young woman in a black blouse and white skirt. He had seen such a woman in O'Connell Street last September when he was up for the All-

Ireland, but she had puffy feet that swelled over her sandal straps, and her back wasn't as straight as Elizabeth's. He wondered what Festus would make of Elizabeth. He once said in Phelan's that all women were at one of two extremes—they were either angels or termagants. They were angels if they belonged to someone else and termagants if they belonged to you. Now, that was a gross oversimplification. For a man who birled a new woman every week, Festus knew nothing about the sex. He, Kevin Hurley, knew more. He knew, for example, that women, like cattle, thrive on good treatment. They should be fed well, properly bedded, and spoken to in loving kindness. If all men treated their women as he treated his dry stock, wives would not lose their sweetness after the first year of marriage. The world was going to the dogs, and men had only themselves to blame for it. They had lost the art of wife management. Now, if he had a wife, he would know what to do with her.

His father was pounding the bedroom floor with his stick when he entered the kitchen.

"I wonder what he can want now," said Maureen, "after me turning him on his left side only twenty minutes ago."

Kevin went upstairs to find the bedclothes on the floor and his father waving his arms like a windmill, struggling to cover his spindle shanks with the sheet.

"I had a terrible dream," he said faintly. "I woke up sweating with the covers on the floor."

Kevin tucked him in and got him a fresh pillow from Maureen's room.

"I dreamt that I died of brucellosis and that Donie Dunne came up to dance a hornpipe on my coffin."

"It was Donie Dunne that died," said Kevin.

"Ah, go 'way."

"Murt Quane told me only ten minutes ago."

"Well, praise be to God and St. Patrick, not to mention

Michael Collins himself. But tell me, tell me, Kevin, what did he die of? Brucellosis?"

"He died because he didn't spend a penny. He died of chronic constipation, or so they say."

"They were always a mean tribe, the Dunnes."

"And to think that a penn'orth of Epsom salts would have shifted the blockage. They took him to Portlaoise Hospital, but he was too far gone. The system was already poisoned."

"Epsom salts, did you say? What he needed was a good rodding. But thanks be to God, for now I can die in peace."

Kevin fled down the stairs from his father's gloating. He was not the sort of man who could sit quietly for half an hour in broad daylight, so he decided to fell an awkward tree to keep himself occupied until Murt arrived.

"I'm going to cut down one of the beeches," he told Maureen. "It's so close to the house that it keeps the light out of the kitchen."

"Isn't there plenty of time for that? Sit down there on the sofa and I'll make you a hot sup in your hand while you're waiting for Murt."

"It isn't only the light. It makes the walls damp and it clogs the gutters. I've been meaning to cut it down all winter."

He got the chain saw from the workshop and walked round the offending beech, pondering how he should fell it. When it was first planted, perhaps it seemed far enough from the sidewall, but as it grew it spread until it overhung the roof. No wonder the slates on the north side were green with moss and fungus.

He cut a neat wedge out of the tree on the side on which he wanted it to fall. Then he went round to the other side and began cutting through the bole. He liked cutting with a chain saw because of the effortless way it went through the wood while it spat sawdust on the uppers of his boots. He was almost there. The tree creaked defiantly as it began to move away from him. With the puttering saw in his hand, he looked up to see the nose of a tractor coming round the corner of the house.

"Look out, Murt," he shouted at the top of his voice.

Weak at the knees, he watched the tree fall in slow motion. He turned off the saw and shouted, "Murt!" again until his throat hurt. Murt looked up, but too late. The tree caught him on the head and shoulder, knocking him out of the seat while the tractor continued its course and crashed into the wall of the unroofed shed.

He ran to Murt, asking him how he was, but there was no audible reply. The tree had fallen on top of him and Kevin was unable to move it. He picked up the chain saw and blindly began to cut through the branches, shouting, "Murt, are you all right?" above the deafening whine of the motor and the blade.

"What on earth are you doing?" Maureen asked from behind.

"The tree, it fell on him."

"Oh, no!"

He grasped Murt's hand and felt the wrist with his fingers.

"Christ! There's no pulse," he said, beginning to cut his way through the remaining branches.

At last he got to the branch that was pressing on Murt's chest. He pulled him out and put him lying on his back, then felt for a heartbeat inside his shirt.

"If he's alive, it's only just," he said. "We'll have to get him to the hospital right away."

Murt's right cheek was gashed and the hair on the back of his head was soaked in blood. A trickle of blood had run down his neck from his cheek, but it was only a trickle.

There were no other signs of injury, yet he was unconscious and his pulse was weak. He stretched him out on the back seat of the car and told Maureen to get in. She got a towel from the house, put it under Murt's head, and rested it on her lap. She sat looking out of the window as he drove mechanically, doing everything without thinking, praying that they would get him to the hospital before it was too late.

"I told you not to cut the tree," Maureen said.

"If only he had brought his new tractor, the cab would have saved him. He had to bring the old one, the one without a cab."

They took Murt to the casualty department and sat alone in a white-emulsioned room with red and green posters.

"You should ring Elizabeth," Maureen said after a while.

The thought of her gave him a start. He went to the telephone in reception but he could not lift the receiver. He got into the car and drove to Larch Lawn like a sleepwalker who could not be woken from his desperate mission.

"I've got terrible news for you," he said when she came to the door. "Murt's been injured. I left him in the hospital, unconscious."

"What injured him?"

"A tree?"

"Did he fall off it?"

"No, I was cutting it and it fell on him."

"You clown, you fool, you eejit." She pummelled his chest with both her fists. "It's just the kind of thing you'd go and do."

He seized her wrists and held her, telling her to get a grip on herself.

"I'll drive you to the hospital," he said.

"No, you won't. I'll drive myself."

He let her go first and followed respectfully at a distance

of fifty yards. He could not take his eyes off the back of her car, telling himself that, though she was in a hurry, she was driving carefully.

Maureen was at the hospital gate with wet eyes.

"He's dead," she sobbed. "The doctor said he never regained consciousness."

4

Kevin was tempted to see in Murt's death the red hand of the Almighty. He had been expecting retribution, but not in the form it had taken. He had expected a tree to fall on himself, not on his friend, which led him to believe that this was only a warning shot, a promise of carnage to come. It was meant to hurt, though. Murt was dear to him, not just a boon companion like Festus O'Flaherty but a mate with whom he shared. O'Flaherty filled a different need in his life. He was a man of fun, whose tirades against women made evenings dwindle into half-hours, but he was at once everyone's friend and no one's friend, because at the centre of his heart was a vacuum or at best a cube of ice. Murt was different. Under his many-coloured cloak of gaiety was a deep seriousness; and though Kevin enjoyed his dry humour, he enjoyed even more his well-pondered opinions on such matters as four-wheel-drive tractors, stubble-burning in autumn, and the best method of sowing winter barley. They had shared machinery and made plans, but they never went for a drink together. And because they had never stretched their legs in a pub, Kevin felt that there were large tracts of life, of their own lives even, on which they had never exchanged an opinion. They had never talked about women, for example, because, whenever they met, cattle, machinery, and the weather seemed more important. Once, admittedly, Murt had mentioned Polly Nangle, B.Agr.Sc., but only to say that she had explained to him something about the pH of soil, about hydrogen-ion concentration, which he had never understood before. His death was such a waste, their friendship a tale of opportunities missed, a fragment without resolution.

As he did his jobs about the farmyard, foddering and bedding the cattle and tidying up for the night, he tried to understand why he expected retribution for incest. Now, if he had killed a man and set fire to his house, he would expect to feel guilt because he had acted against society, because he had committed a crime against the person and violated another man's property rights, both of them offences punishable by law. But in going to bed with his all-too-willing sister he was not acting against the interest of society; yet he felt as if he had done something abhorrent to humanity as well as God. Maureen and he were consenting adults. He had not inveigled her to his bed, as might a dirty old father his innocent daughter. She had come of her own accord.

Why the taboo against sexual relations within the family? Such knowledge harmed no one, and it shed a ray of warmth on lives that had known too much cold. Festus once said that in every country of the world, even in countries where cannibalism was still practised, incest was forbidden; that even a just ruler in ancient Babylonia, someone called Hammurabi, had made incest a capital offence; that in the course of human history it was permitted only here and there among certain groups—among the royal families of ancient

Egypt and Peru, for example. It was all very confusing. His intellect told him that sexual intercourse with his sister could be no more harmful than a good rough tumble with a black woman from Timbuktu. Yet his intellect was like chaff in the wind compared with the insistent force of his feelings, which now discoloured his life as an inky cloud would drain the brightness from the greens and blues of Slieve Bloom.

Now there was a further cloud. If he had not committed incest, Murt would still be alive. Maureen would not have been pregnant; and if she had not been pregnant, he would not have asked Murt to help him with the girders on that particular day. No one knew that except Maureen and himself, but Elizabeth Quane may have sensed it. She had not spoken to him since her brother's death. At the wake she had ignored him, and at the graveside she had turned her straight back on his obvious distress.

He was now back on square one. Maureen was still pregnant, and he still had not found her a man.

"What will we do now?" she asked over dinner as soon as Murt was decently buried.

"I'm thinking," he said.

"You'll have to think quickly. In a month or two I'll look as heavy as I feel."

"I've solved our problem," he told her the following day.

"Tell me first and then I'll tell you if I agree."

"We've been going about this the wrong way, trying to find a man who would take a fancy to you."

"Thank you very much!"

"What we need is a man who will live here with us, and then it will not matter if he takes a fancy to you or not."

"Why should anyone want to live with us?"

"I'll pay him. What I'm saying is that I'll hire a farm labourer to help me out."

"The depth of winter is a strange time to hire a farm labourer."

"Don't worry, I'll find plenty for him to do. There's the drainage not to mention sixty acres of bog to reclaim."

"And what will I have to do?"

"You'll have to take an interest in him and make him take an interest in you."

"But I thought you said that didn't matter?"

"It would be better if he gave you a bit of a tumble, and I'm sure that's something you can arrange. But if he doesn't, it won't be the end of the world. The neighbours are bound to jump to the wrong conclusion."

"They will think the child is his?"

"That's right."

"It will look bad for me. People will call me a trollop."

"Better to be called a trollop than to end up in prison."

"You're a cruel man, Kevin, just like your father, not very sensitive."

"The world has little use for sensitivity. You know, as I was crushing oats yesterday, I thought I was looking at life and what it does to you. I picked up a handful of the crushed oats and I felt like God with a platoon of broken men in his fist, all of them pummelled and flattened, waiting to be consumed. Every one of us is consumed—by life, by death, by the earth itself."

They spent an hour after dinner discussing likely candidates. She was very choosy, but at last they managed to settle on a short list of four. During the following week he went to Killage three times and to two Masses on Sunday in order to meet them, but every man jack of them turned him down. They all had other fish to fry.

On the following Saturday he was having his weekly drink in Phelan's with Festus O'Flaherty when a man from the edge of town called Billy Snoddy came across to them.

"You're a stranger here," said Festus.

"I only came in to see Kevin."

"What can I do for you?" Kevin asked.

"I hear you're looking for a man. If you are, I'm for hire."

"He doesn't want a man, not at this time of year," said Festus. "What he wants is a husband for his sister. You'd better look out, Snoddy. If you're not careful, you'll be hanged, drawn, and betrothed before you know where you are."

They all laughed, Kevin more loudly than the other two.

He seemed to remember that Maureen had been out with Billy Snoddy when she was a girl, but he felt that now she might consider him too old. He was at least fifty, and Maureen, he knew, fancied younger men like Murt. He decided to play for time, to discuss the matter with her before taking him on.

"It's true I'm looking for a man. I've asked someone already, and he said he'd let me know tomorrow. If he doesn't say yes, the job is yours. What Mass do you go to on Sunday?"

"Late Mass in Killage."

"I'll see you outside the chapel gate afterwards."

Maureen was baking bread for the morning when he got home.

"I met Billy Snoddy in Phelan's," he told her.

"Going into Phelan's with the quality, is he? My, my, he has come up in the world."

"He wants to come to work for us—he heard I was looking for a man."

"Oh, no!" she said, putting her flour-whitened hands to her face.

"He's the last chance."

"He was born in soot and reared in smoke, his father a cottager who never did a day's work."

"You've been out with him before, haven't you?"

"I was only a scutcher then, no more than fifteen. But have you thought of this? Is there e'er a lep left in him?"

"That doesn't matter if people think there is."

"What did you tell him?"

"I said I'd see him after late Mass tomorrow."

"Tell him what you like."

"I'll tell him to come then," he said, beginning to unlace his shoes.

"It's an odd coincidence," she said. "He crossed my mind just before you came in. I happened to be thinking that now you never see a man with an overcoat on the handlebars of his bicycle."

"That's because there are no bicycles."

"When we were growing up, all courtin' men used to carry an overcoat on the handlebars to spread under the girl, and the better-off ones used to have two—one to wear if it rained and one to lie on. The way I came to think of Billy Snoddy was that he always carried two, and he only a cottager's son. I remember one evening meeting him at Dooley's Cross and he wearing a heavy overcoat and a heavier one rolled over the handlebars. We walked towards Gravel and went into Lar Teeling's old turf shed near the next cross. It was a handy shed. A lot of people used to go in there for all sorts of reasons. We were kissin' in the corner when he went out to his bicycle for his spare overcoat to spread on the floor. He lit a match to see what he was doing, and there between his feet was a filthy thing as thick as a cable. We moved to the opposite corner and lay on his overcoat, but I couldn't concentrate. I kept laughin' an' gigglin' till he lost all patience. 'What's come over you?' he asked 'It's the Lad in the Corner,' I said, and laughed even louder. From that evening I could never go out with him again. And whenever I saw him on his bicycle with two heavy overcoats, I would burst out laughing at the Lad in the Corner."

"You'll have memories in common, then."

"Memories that will lead to nothing good. He was buckin' mad with me when I gave him up. If he's a bachelor today, it's because of me—"

"—and the Lad in the Corner."

"I would prefer someone who never had any feeling for me. It would be simpler and more natural."

Billy Snoddy came the following week. Because he had worked all his life as a farmhand and never had a house of his own, he had to sleep at Clonglass in the small bedroom next to their father's. Kevin disliked him from the start, if only because he destroyed by his mere presence the unthinking sense of peace Kevin used to feel at mealtimes. Kevin enjoyed his food. In particular, he enjoyed breakfast, which he prepared himself and ate alone before Maureen got up, and which invariably consisted of cold beef with mustard, cold baked beans, and soda bread washed down with two mugs of strong, sweet tea. He would eat after feeding the cattle, while he listened to the news and weather forecast on the radio and threw bread crusts to Pup, who sat on his haunches begging for more. He did not blame Maureen for being a late riser. He preferred to make his own breakfast, because he liked to eat in silence so early in the morning. At dinnertime he had Maureen for company, but her unceasing chatter complemented rather than vexed his thoughts. She was the kind of conversationalist who is essentially a monologist. To enjoy a "conversation," she merely required a sympathetic presence, and if, as sometimes happened, her observations required a reply, she was willing to repeat herself twice or even three times without discouragement.

Billy Snoddy changed all that. He got up at the same

time as Kevin and tried to make small talk over breakfast when Kevin wished for silence. At dinnertime he would sit at the far end of the table looking from brother to sister and back again, never missing an inflexion or even the cast of an eye. He seemed to find as much meaning in silence as in speech, so that Kevin ruefully told himself that silence at table was no longer golden but glaringly pregnant.

Snoddy was an unprepossessing bugger. Small and thin with lank jaws that showed through his black stubble, he had the eyes and mouth of a frightened frog. The eyes stood out as if threatening to forsake their sockets, and the skin under his chin, which hung loosely like a gobbler's wattles, inflated and deflated when he swallowed. As he always swallowed between sentences, the process of inflation and deflation and the corresponding up-and-down movement of his Adam's apple were never ending. In addition, he was unclean in his habits. His fingernails were dirty, and his black hair, for lack of washing, lay flat and thick on his crown like lodged wheat after a rainstorm. His clothes shone with the glazed grime of a dozen seasons, and the holed sweater which he wore beneath his jacket looked the worse for having been used as a hand towel after meals. But what Kevin noticed most was none of those things but his small white teeth with gaping interstices between.

His table manners were far from being his greatest social asset. He ate with lips apart so that you could see the un-chewed food between his teeth, and in his haste to gorge himself he refused to acknowledge that his knife and fork had been manufactured for different functions. After the first day Kevin decided that Snoddy had more in common with cer-tain four-footed animals than with himself. By careful, though not objective, observation, he discovered that if Snoddy swallowed a mouthful of food before starting a sen-tence, it would miraculously reappear in his mouth at the end of it. This could only be explained as a form of rumination, a chewing of the cud. He would then proceed to chew the bolus he had previously swallowed before embarking on another sentence, which showed at least an unerring appreciation of where one sentence ended and another began. However, what interested Kevin most, and might also interest a zoologist or a vet, was that he chewed quickly with the same sideways movement of the jaw as a wether, not with the slow deliberation of a bullock.

The idea of Snoddy having several stomachs fascinated Kevin so much that he was soon led to wonder about his food conversion rate. Kevin once had a bullock that achieved a liveweight gain of 3.97 pounds a day over 400 days, but Snoddy was hardly in that league. He was clearly an inefficient feeder. For dinner he would demolish six thick slices of beef without mustard, a piled-up platter of parsnips and turnips and perhaps over six pounds of potatoes. Yet he was as thin as a rake. Though his conversion efficiency rate was low, it was possible that he would give a surprisingly good result in the abattoir. A high growth rate wasn't everything. Lean meat and a high kill-out at slaughter were equally, perhaps more, desirable.

Kevin observed him closely with Maureen, but in his conversation he could find no hint of nostalgia for the girl who had forsaken him because of the Lad in the Corner more than twenty years ago. He would look at her sadly with frog's eyes, lick his lips like an anteater, and deliver himself of wise sayings with the detachment of a man who doesn't believe in them. Maureen watched television in the evenings, but Snoddy scorned the little screen, which, he said, reduced everyone to the level of cattle ticks—all parasitic receptivity. When Kevin demanded to know if these ticks produce redwater fever in the television comedians on whom they feed, Snoddy buried himself in *The Leinster Express* and refused to be drawn. He was a tireless reader of newspapers, especially local newspapers, and it was one of his axioms that a newspaper, no matter how old, is new if you have not read it before. He was a good farmhand, though. And to some extent that made up for the sense of unease with which he filled Kevin in his own kitchen.

After two weeks Maureen told Kevin that Snoddy had made a pass at her in the dairy.

"What kind of pass?" he asked, aware of the morbidity of his interest.

"He put his arm round me like that when I was mixing the hens' feed, and then he kissed me on the back of the neck."

"What a strange place to kiss a woman. Do you think he's all right?"

"Oh, yes," she said. "When I pretended not to notice, he put his hand up my skirt."

"And did you notice then?"

"I told him to remove his hand or I'd give him a good goosing."

"I think it's time I 'discovered' you both in bed together. When you're ready, let me know the day. I'll say I'm going into Killage for something, but instead of going all the way to town, I'll turn at Quane's gate and drive back after fifteen minutes. By then you'll both be in bed. I'll tiptoe upstairs and solve our little problem."

"Do I have to go to bed with him?"

"Yes, but you don't have to go the whole hog if you don't want to."

"But if I don't go the whole hog . . ."

"Do what you think most enjoyable, because that is what will vex you least."

Two days later, after a wink from Maureen, he said that he was going into town for a new battery for the tractor. It was a bright, cold day at the beginning of February, and as he drove down the lane with mischievous joy in his heart, he felt the flutter of youthful excitement, as if life were well worth living, as if he had recovered the sense of immortality he used to feel in springtime at eighteen. The young buds were red and green on the hedges, and a watery sun struck through a cloud at the flat head of Slieve Bloom. He switched on the car radio and laughed as he heard his favourite ballad singer rendering:

> "O, I will and I must get married
> For the humour is on me now."

As he turned at Quane's gate, Elizabeth came down the drive with her big black Labrador at heel. In sudden confusion, he raised his hand and she signalled to him to wait.

"I was going into town for a new battery when I discovered that I'd forgotten my wallet," he said, somehow constrained to explain his appearance at her gate.

"So you've got to go home again?" She smiled. "If you like, you can borrow the money from me and pay me back next time you're passing."

Her talk was so unlike Murt's, so alien in its perfection, that he felt he must escape before he exposed the black core of his heart.

"It's all right. It will only take me five minutes to nip back home."

"I'm sorry about the way I behaved over Murt's death. I wasn't myself under the shock."

She was standing with her ringless hand on the door handle of his car. As he noted the big brown buttons of her herringbone overcoat and the sad face of her bitch Labrador, he wished that he had turned at Lalor's.

"Grief does strange things to us all," he said.

"Will you come up to the house for a minute? I've got something to show you."

He got out of the car and walked with her up the drive, aware of her strong, flat shoes—nurse's shoes—and the upward tilt of her chin. Her features were clean-cut rather than softly pretty, and her straight back hinted at reserves of character and the lack of self-knowledge that often accompanies self-will. She took off her overcoat in the hallway to reveal a tight-fitting blue skirt and jacket with a frilly white blouse underneath. He sat at the kitchen table as he used to do when Murt was alive, and she came back from the parlour and laid an official-looking document on the table before him.

"It's Murt's will," she said. "He made it six months before he died, a strange thing for a young man to do. It was as if he had sensed that he wasn't long for this world. He left the land and the house to me, and he left you the right to walk in the Grove whenever you take the vagary. There's the clause. Read it yourself and see."

She went to the dresser and, without asking him, poured him a glass of ale and a schooner of dry sherry for herself.

"He was a deep man," she said, sitting down opposite him. "But you knew him well."

"We were friends."

"He was an intelligent man, but he never talked about anything except farming. That's why I used to make fun of you both about early bite and back-end grazing."

"We realized that."

"What did you and he talk about when you were alone?"

"Farming."

"Anything else?"

"The weather—but only when it was bad."

"And you still were the best of friends. I remember how he once said that though you were a hard worker no one ever saw you in a hurry."

"He was a hard worker himself."

"When I was in Dublin, I used to send him books about farming. They're still on a shelf in the parlour."

"He never told me that."

"You can borrow them if you like."

"I'm not much of a reader."

"Did he ever talk about his girl friend—what's her name?"

"Polly Nangle. Only once to say that she had told him about the pH of soil."

"Maybe he went out with her because of her knowledge."

"I wouldn't know."

He felt as if he had fallen under a spell, as if he had some precious knowledge unbeknown to himself which only Elizabeth could bring to life in him. He took a long, slow sip from his glass, wondering what he or she would say next. The clock was ticking on the wall, the cat was asleep on the settee, Billy Snoddy was tumbling Maureen, and he felt stuck to his chair.

"How are you coping with the farm?" he asked.

"I have a good foreman, John Noonan, but I keep an eye on him. I feel I shouldn't leave anything to chance."

"I'd be only too pleased to help if I could."

"If I'm ever in doubt about anything, I'll know where to go."

She got up and placed her empty glass on the drainer by the sink, breaking the spell that bound him. He hurried to the car and drove back furiously to Clonglass. As he came through the second gate, he saw Snoddy leave the house with the peak of his cap turned backwards.

"You eejit," yelled Maureen when he entered the kitchen.

"I went down to Quane's to turn, and I had to change a wheel at Sheridan's on the way back."

"You're steeped in luck, aren't you?"

"You lay with him, then?"

"I did."

"Did you do the bold thing?"

"I'm not tellin'. I don't think it's good for you to know."

"I must know. Are you in the clear or not?"

"I'm in the clear."

"I could catch you both tomorrow if you like."

"Once is enough."

"You don't sound like a satisfied customer."

"He was out of practice. He came too soon."

He strode out of the kitchen with a sense of outrage. Hearing that they had done the bold thing washed over him like gentle river water, but the knowledge that he'd come too quickly pummelled and winded him like an Atlantic roller off the coast of Clare. He avoided Snoddy all afternoon and had his tea in silence while Maureen reminisced and Snoddy indulged his taste for antiphonal conundrums.

"I think the young people of today miss all the fun of growing up because they can do anything that comes into their heads," said Maureen.

"But they soon find out that anything is nothing," said Snoddy.

"When we were growing up," said Maureen, "it took a week of cajolin' and slootherin' to get permission out of Mammy to go to a dance. But if it weren't for her, God rest her soul, neither Concepta nor myself would ever have had a date, because His Dotage upstairs couldn't bear the thought of a man putting his hand up his daughter's skirt."

"It's a wise man who knows the contents of his daughter's drawers," said Snoddy.

"I was lucky in a way," Maureen continued. "Concepta was younger than me, but Mammy trusted her because she wouldn't be seen dead with a farmer. And since the only men around were farmers, Mammy knew that as long as I stayed with Concepta I'd be safe. She let us go to one dance a week provided we went to confession on Saturdays, but a week is a long time if you're fifteen and dying for a squeeze. That's why I'd use the cows as an excuse to get out of the house. In summer I used to drive them from the moor every evening at six for milking, and then I used to drive them back at eight. That was my opportunity of the day. I used to nip down the road to Dooley's Cross to see if Robert Kirwan was waiting, but I could only stay twenty minutes in case His Dotage discovered I was missing. On Sunday nights Mammy would let us go to the dance unbeknown to him. We would pretend to go to bed, and then we would throw our good clothes out the bedroom window, climb down the drainpipe, and change in the turf shed behind the house. When we came back after midnight, we had to make sure that Daddy didn't see us. Mammy would leave the parlour window open for us, and if Daddy was still up she would ask him to go out for a skib of turf so that we could sneak upstairs while his back was turned. Concepta never did any business at dances, but I always made hay while the moon shone, and Concepta would stand like a policeman ten yards away saying every five minutes, 'Whatever are you doing now, Maureen?'"

"It was a life of innocence," said Snoddy. "A squeeze was worth a herd of cattle, but now the whole hog isn't worth a fart. We're all victims of sexual inflation, and the worst hit are those on fixed incomes."

Kevin covered his beef with mustard and said nothing. He had told himself that he did not give a damn about Maureen and Snoddy, but he was hurt by the discovery that he knew so little about himself.

After dinner the following day, he went upstairs to turn his father in the bed.

"Have you ever heard the saying 'three acres and a pig'?" the old bugger grunted.

"I've heard of 'three acres and a cow,'" said Kevin.

"No, that's an English phrase, but 'three acres and a pig' is Spanish. It was invented by no less a Spaniard than De Valera. You see, he was going to divide all Ireland into two provinces. In one of them he was going to put all the Catholics with three acres and a pig apiece, and in the other he was going to put all the Protestants with three acres and a horse."

"I've never heard of it," said Kevin.

"To give him his due, it was good politics. Pigs, you see, breed more quickly and grow faster than horses, and his intention was that the Catholics would get richer and richer and the Protestants poorer and poorer, because a sow will drop a litter of twelve or more twice a year whereas a mare will take eleven months over one foal. Do you see the low Mediterranean cunning of the bastard? Oh, it was not by accident that Michael Collins got shot in the back at Beal na Blath."

"I've never heard of that either."

"What did they teach you in school? You see, De Valera had pigs on the brain. It was pigs, not the treaty, that was behind the Civil War. De Valera believed in dry feeding, but Griffith, Collins, Duggan, Barton, and Duffy were all skimmilk men. The unanswerable question is whether the five of them were plenipotentiaries or just delegates, but if you want to know the answer I'll tell you."

"I left the kettle on the hotplate. I must take it off before it boils dry."

He went to the door, but his father's phlegm-muffled voice still held him. "When are you going to take a woman to yourself?" he demanded.

"Any day now, Daddy. I'm only waiting for Miss Riche-ffrench O'Carroll."

"It's not natural for a man to live alone. Even Dev took a woman to himself, and he was the most unnatural man that ever batted an eyelid. Though he looked like the devil himself in a black overcoat—Devilera was no nickname—he managed to lure a woman to his bed, a wee fairy of a thing with a scared look, but a woman with a woman's accoutrements for all that. Now, that's more than you've done. All you've ever ridden is the bloody mare, and I'll bet you never rode her bareback—"

"I can hear the kettle boiling over."

He hurried out of the room and bumped against Maureen, who looked as if she had been eavesdropping.

"He's gone soft in the head, the oul' divil. He's now saying that Dev murdered Michael Collins."

"You know what the doctor said. We mustn't contradict him."

"I didn't contradict him. I just bit on the bullet."

"Never mind him Kevin. With any luck he'll be joining Dev and Collins very soon."

She put an arm round his waist and led him into her bedroom. "I'm in a bad way, Kevin."

"Don't worry. I'll make sure to catch you at it next time."

"It's not that."

"What is it, then?"

"I'm dying for a rub of the relic. I'm so far gone that even a rub would do."

To unzip his reliquary was the last thing he wished for, so he sat on the edge of the bed, seized by physical and mental exhaustion. He wanted to walk out of the house and forget about his reprobate of a father, his whore of a sister, and the evil-smelling Snoddy. He wanted to walk down the lane and into the Grove, sit in silence under a tree, and look at a blue sky through black branches. Playfully, she pushed him back on the bed and began to undo his shoelaces.

"What about Snoddy?" he asked in sudden inspiration.

"He went down the lane whistling ten minutes ago."

"And what was he whistling?"

"I meet a maid in the greenwood shade at the dawning of the day."

"You've made him a very happy man," he said as she pulled off his trousers.

They lay in each other's arms for ten minutes while the cold bed thawed.

"Where is it?" she asked as she rummaged in his underpants.

"Don't rush me. I'm always slow to start in cold weather."

She kissed him with the inside of her lips, drawing his tongue into her mouth, where it was immediately set upon by her own. Their tongues were like gamecocks, darting and retreating and rising again to the attack, but still he could not take his mind off the maid in the greenwood shade and the whistling of Billy Snoddy.

"He doesn't have to dance a jig," she said. "She's so far gone that if you lay him against her it will be enough."

The bedroom door creaked, and the lean face of Billy Snoddy seemed transfixed for a moment on the jamb.

"I'm afraid I'm late," he said and closed the door, his high-pitched voice rising in song:

> "With milking pail she sought the vale,
> And bright her charms' display;
> Outshining far the morning star
> At the dawning of the day."

Kevin jumped out of bed and the voice in the corridor faded away.

"I'm afraid it's not my week," said Maureen, putting the pillow over her head.

5

"We understand each other, you and me," said Billy Snoddy. "And as long as we understand each other, nothing can go wrong."

They had put the girders and purlins in position and on top them wire netting and a layer of felt. All was ready for the corrugated iron sheeting which was to form the roof of the shed.

Kevin refused to answer, and Snoddy went down the ladder for the bolts. He had his back to Kevin, stooping over a cardboard box, and for a moment Kevin's mind whirled on the edge of blackness. It would have been so easy to drop the edge of the corrugated sheet on Snoddy's neck, but the moment passed and the sheet remained in his hand. An accident perhaps, an accident on a farm which seemed to be jinxed.

"We're both men of the world," said Snoddy, coming up the ladder. "And men of the world never show surprise. They know the world but the world doesn't know them."

"Never mind the philosophy, just hand me the drill."

"If the world got to know what a man of the world was really like, it might turn its back on him."

Kevin took the drill from Snoddy, bitterly regretting that he had not dropped the iron sheet on his neck. He would be insufferable now, his conversation more mysterious than ever. But he, Kevin, would have to keep a grip on himself, pretend that what Snoddy knew did not matter. If Snoddy got the idea that he was afraid of him, that would be the end. Though Snoddy was a hard worker, he might conceivably wish for a sinecure and security for the rest of his life. There was no doubt that he would exact a price for the concealment of his ill-gotten knowledge. But what price?

Kevin was uneasy, because he could not see Snoddy as he would a bullock or a tractor. He felt, indeed he knew, that the man he saw was not the real man at all. It was as if the light kept changing so that the colours beguiled the eye and the contours of the object remained unseen. One moment he saw Snoddy as his salvation, as the man who would take Maureen off his hands and rid him of his heart-eating guilt; and the next he would squirm at the thought of Maureen in bed with him, his twin sister making love to a man with a rumen, reticulum, omasum, and abomasum. It seemed to him that he must have an hour of quiet to put distance between himself and the Abominable Ruminant. He told him that he was going to Killage for more bolts and drove off in his dung-spangled Mercedes, glad to be alone. About half a mile down the road he parked the car in the entrance of a disused laneway and walked up the darkly enclosed path to the Grove, the entanglement of trees and bushes on each side entwining overhead, reminding him of one of his oldest memories, the day he saw the pooka on horseback.

He must have been about four—he certainly was no more because the Grove still belonged to his father—when he wandered down the road on a windy October day to pick blackberries and hazelnuts. The wind was so strong that he told himself that the branches were galloping up and down, and then he heard real galloping and a tall, straight-backed man with a moustache passed him on horseback, the reins in one hand and a long-legged barstool in the other. As he approached the corner, he reined in quickly and vanished straight through the hedge. Kevin took the shadowy path that led to the Grove, stopping every now and then to pick a blackberry or a sloe while the lukewarm sun gave the look of death to the yellowing leaves. Suddenly he stopped behind a big tree to find the dismounted horseman tying the reins to an overhanging branch only ten feet away. Then he placed the barstool behind the horse and got up on it while he held the horse's tail in his hand. Next the man's trousers fell to his ankles, the horse raised his head, and its penis grew like a stout blackthorn with great rings along its length. Kevin could not see what the man was doing to the horse, but whatever it was the horse was enjoying it, because it turned round and bit its shoulder in near ecstasy. Just then a wood pigeon broke cover with a clatter and Kevin took to his heels in terror. As he reached the road, he heard the thud of hooves on soft turf behind him and he took refuge in the hedge, keeping his head well down and grasping his paper bag of nuts and blackberries as if it were a magic shield. Then the horse was on the road, because the thudding changed to a ringing clip-clop that struck terror into his pounding heart. He looked up from under a branch and saw the man once more in the saddle, straight-backed and moustached with a green hat on his head, the reins in his left hand and the stool in the other.

He ran all the way home, and when he told his mother that he'd seen the pooka on a horse, she said that he was a regular visitor to Clonglass, that he was looking for boys who stayed out late picking blackberries. He never told anyone else about the pooka, but he thought about it every day because it puzzled him more than the schoolmaster's arithmetic. He was still puzzled by it. Now he did not know if he'd seen it or imagined it, because like many early "memories" it could have been the result of suggestion rather than experience. If he had not seen it, had he imagined it because he was inherently evil? And if he had seen it, why had the horseman chosen a stallion rather than a mare, and why did the stallion get an erection so quickly after the man got up on the stool? Once, when Festus O'Flaherty was very drunk, Kevin told him that he had heard the story from a tinker at a horse fair in Galway, and when he asked Festus why the stallion had got an erection, Festus laughed as if Kevin were a simpleton. Though he was drunk, he did not forget the story. In fact, he was so taken with the idea of a horseman with a barstool riding about the Irish midlands that he used to ask Kevin every now and then to refresh his memory.

"Tell me the story of the Hippophilous Pooka," he would say. And then he'd laugh till the froth shook on the pint of stout in his hand.

Because of what he had seen or imagined, the Grove was a place of mystery to Kevin. The weak February sun struck obliquely across the bare branches, and here and there a few green plants were starting to peep through the winter carpet of dead leaves. The dead leaves were crisp underfoot, and the green plants anaemic as if their hold on life was not yet strong. He went straight to the Pooka Tree, sat on a decaying log, and rested his back against the trunk. Words came to him from a distance, and he did not know what they were until he heard the sound of them on his lips:

"What we call the comforts of life are an illusion. My land, my cattle, my house, my tractors, my sister, my Saturday evenings with Festus in Phelan's—none of them truly belongs to me. Land is just waiting to swallow you, cattle die, tractors rust, Maureen could marry Snoddy, and Festus could go back to Connemara."

A long, ringed earthworm crawled from under a dead leaf between his legs. Compared with a man, it was a low form of life, barely warm, barely sensible. Yet, when you thought of human life as it might be, you realized that an earthworm was only a little less than a man. They both fell so short of the ideal that only a fool or a university professor would wish to differentiate between them.

"I am impotent in my own house. I should horsewhip Snoddy, but I won't. I should take him by the scruff of the neck and boot him down the lane as far as the lower gate, but I won't. I can't. I can only sit tight, breathe quietly, do nothing. Three years ago I would have strangled him for talking to me like that, but that was before Mother died, before Maureen. . ."

For a long time his mother had had a pain in her stomach, especially after meals, but still she refused to go to the doctor. He lost patience finally, and on the next mart day he called on Dr. Blizzard.

"Bring her to the surgery tomorrow afternoon. I'm free after four," Blizzard said.

"But she won't come. She's headstrong, always was, and my father is too old to get round her any more."

"I'll call in to see her, then," said Blizzard, placing the tips of his lady fingers together to form a little cone.

Blizzard arrived in the farmyard the following afternoon, picking his steps between the car and the house, lifting his feet higher than necessary, lifting them like a spancelled gander on ice.

"I was passing and I called in," he said to Kevin's mother. "I heard a few weeks ago that you were having pains in the tummy and I wondered if they had gone away."

She was reluctant to let him examine her, but finally she

73

asked him to come into the parlour while Kevin and Maureen waited in the kitchen.

Kevin accompanied Dr. Blizzard to his car. Though the day was warm, he was wearing a long tweed overcoat; and though he walked daintily, there were two specks of slurry on his neatly pointed patent-leather shoes. Kevin led him towards a cake of cow dung in the yard, but he gave it as wide a berth as if it had been an infectious disease. Kevin could not help feeling that vets were more human, that for their sins of pride and pomposity doctors should be made to treat cattle.

"She has a lump the size of a horse chestnut on the left side of her abdomen," Blizzard said without looking at Kevin. He was making a comparative study of his car keys while the breeze blew intimations of his aftershave in Kevin's direction.

"What can it be?" Kevin asked.

"It's not for me to say. She will have to go to hospital for an examination."

"What could it be?"

"It's too early to say."

"But surely you must have some idea."

"It could be a tumour," Dr. Blizzard said, flicking a greenfly off his grey herringbone sleeve. Kevin cursed him for a coward and persisted.

"Could it be the bucko?"

"The bucko?"

"Cancer."

"It could. But on the other hand it could be a benign tumour—harmless, not malignant. We shan't know until we've had the results of the X ray."

Dr. Blizzard was tall and narrow-chested, with an academic stoop that gave him an air of absent-minded condescension. It was not his academic stoop that made women tingle, however, but his syrupy bass, which had reassured many a patient who had thought herself beyond reassurance. Kevin listened to his basso profundo and was not reassured.

"We mustn't leap to premature conclusions." Dr. Blizzard smiled. "I'll ring the hospital as soon as I get home."

Kevin wondered why he had thought it necessary to smile. A vet wouldn't smile at a Hereford heifer, however pretty, before injecting her, and neither would the A.I. man. But perhaps he remembered the story of the king who invariably executed bearers of bad news.

A month later he took his mother to hospital and went out to the pub while she was having a barium meal and X rays. When he came back, a sweet-smelling nurse took him to see an anxious young doctor.

"The results are indeterminate," he said. "In other words, we still don't know. We know it's a tumour. About that there can be no doubt, but whether it's malignant or benign is something the plates don't show."

He spoke carelessly, like a man who despised mere words, and kept one hand in the pocket of his white coat as if he were covering Kevin with a handgun. Another doctor, Kevin thought, who could do with a few basic lessons in the manger-side manner from a practising vet.

"What do we do now?" Kevin asked.

"She must have an operation."

"Is it necessary?"

"It's the only way we can find out the truth."

"What if the truth is cancer?"

"The surgeon would have to remove the tumour and the parts of the intestines to which the cancer has spread. In some cases it is necessary to close the rectum, but there is no point in theorizing. We must wait and see."

"What have you told her?"

"I did not want to alarm her unnecessarily. I told her

that she must have an exploratory operation, that we suspect gallstones in the bile duct."

When he told his father the news, he said that the anxious young doctor was right, that they must keep the truth from her at all costs. She did not want to have the operation, especially when she heard that she would have to go to Dublin.

"More people from this parish went up to Dublin than ever came back," she commented with effortless accuracy, but thanks to Dr. Blizzard's basso profundo Kevin found himself driving her to the capital on a Tuesday in July. The nurse told him that they would operate on the following Friday, so he said goodbye to his mother, telling her that he would visit her before the operation. He disliked leaving her to the mercies of briskly impersonal nurses, but he had his jobs to do and there was no one to do them for him. He drove up to Dublin again on Friday, and the same nurse told him that his mother had been on the operating table for the last hour.

"How long will it take?" he asked.

"It could take another three hours," she said.

He sat in the waiting room turning over the pages of a women's magazine. The nurse came back and rubbed one leg against the other by the door.

"The operation didn't take as long as we expected. The surgeon would like to see you."

"Is that good news or bad news?"

"The surgeon will tell you," she said, leading the way.

The surgeon was a young man who exercised the fingers of one hand against the palm of the other as he spoke. Kevin had no idea that a surgeon could be so young, younger than himself. He had always imagined surgeons to be old and experienced, venerable as mitred bishops among a flurry of deacons.

"Complications, complications," said the surgeon.

"Will she live?" Kevin asked.

"Let me put it this way. She won't die yet."

"What's wrong with her?"

"She has cancer of the large intestine. It had spread all over. The liver is also affected. There is nothing we can do except to try to reduce her suffering."

"How long does she have to live?"

"Three months, maybe four."

"Will it be painful?"

"It is the most painful cancer there is."

As a child he would go into her bedroom in the mornings and lie between her and his father. He would ask her what he had been like as a baby, and she would tell him that when he cried in the night she would take him into her warm bed and put him lying in the middle and tickle his little feet.

"And what would I do then?" he would ask.

"You would drink milk from my breasts."

He asked her that question again and again because of the pleasure he got from the reply, from the world of wonder and warmth it invoked. One morning, when she was sleeping alone in bed, he climbed in beside her and put his mouth to her breast. She woke at once and pushed him rudely away, as if he were no longer her son, as if he had turned himself into an eternal stranger.

"I only wanted a drink of milk," he said.

"You're too old to be suckled."

"Why?"

"You've got teeth now. If I suckled you now, you'd hurt me."

It seemed a reasonable answer, but he could not forget the cast of horror in her eyes. She never touched him willingly after that, and when he would put his arms round her waist as she kneaded dough in the kitchen, she would take his hands and push him firmly away. She would fondle Maureen and Concepta when they came home from school, but she was determined to keep him at arm's length. It was as if he had committed an unforgivable sin that obliterated forever the world of wonder and warmth he had glimpsed in her bed. At nine he took to sleepwalking at night, but she locked her bedroom door so that he would wake, so she said, when he could not open it.

They buried her in Killage churchyard on a wet November day with rain and mist enclosing the small group round the grave. As the first shovelfuls of earth drummed on the coffin, a blackened leaf fell on the engraved plate. After the funeral one of the neighbours who was in a hurry gave Maureen a lift home while Kevin stood a drink for the others in the nearest pub. A few of the neighbours came home with him and they had another drink in the kitchen while outside the rain closed in over the hedges. They did not talk of disease or death but of winter cereals and spring calving, and Kevin waited patiently for them to go, because he did not like drinking in the middle of the day. At last a patch of brightness appeared like a star in the west, and one of the neighbours said that he had a few jobs to do before nightfall. Kevin went to the door and watched the last of them going through the first gate.

"They're not too drunk," he said to himself. "They remembered to close the gate behind them."

He went into the parlour and Maureen rushed to him and pressed her wet face against his chest. He stood like a pillar with his arms by his sides while she gripped him round the waist and shook with sobs. She was shorter than he, and he looked out of the window over her head, imagining the field beyond the Red Gate and the field behind that again, waiting until he could decently move away. The field behind the Red Gate was lea land and the field beyond that was under winter barley, but Maureen clung to him till he could feel nothing but the pressure of her groin and the heaving of her breasts from sobbing. He tried to think of winter barley yellowing because of nitrogen deficiency, only to find himself worrying lest she should feel the hard head of his erection through his trousers. Then she clasped him round the neck and drew his face down over her own, kissing him full on the lips until he backed away as if he had lost his balance.

"Put on the kettle and make a drop of tea while I have a look at Henry," he said.

There was no need to have a look at Henry, so he walked through the Red Gate, up the lea field, and pulled a switch from a laburnum to slash against his trouser leg. His winter barley showed no signs of yellowing and the head-lands showed no signs of slugs. It occurred to him that those were problems that could be solved by top dressing and slug pellets, whereas the dark stirring in his bones was as deep-seated as life itself. Within the space of three minutes in the parlour, Maureen had shown him the thin partition that divides order from chaos. Yesterday, though it had been taken up with visitors to the wake and arrangements for the funeral, had been the essence of order, but today bore the seeds of nightmare. All afternoon he could not put his sister from his thoughts, and it seemed to him that he had omitted to think about her before only because he had been blind to the swing of his own nature. He now knew that if he had made the "wrong" move in the parlour he would have found himself on top of her on the settee. The urgency of her kissing told him that there was no doubt about her intention, but he had rejected her, and now the opportunity for probing the darkness in them both might never arise again. He did not know whether he should feel glad or sad. One moment he felt that he had lost the chance to bring back wonder and warmth to his life, and the next he told himself that what he had sensed within him was so horrifying that it did not bear thinking about.

As he foddered the calves, he told himself that he was being foolish, that the moment of madness was truly over. He would not approach her, in case she should reject him, and she would not approach him again, lest he reject her a second time. Often he had wondered how a man and a woman, any man and woman, go to bed together for the first time. Though they may not have been brought up in an atmosphere of sexual taboos, they will be aware of the inviolable sovereignty by which each person owns himself and of the violence of the invasion of one body by another. For that reason they probably do not appoint a day or night in advance and write it down in their diaries. No, it must surely happen more spontaneously. They are together in the dark, like earthworms, one against the other, and in their ego-obliterating reverie they both move like sleepwalkers in the same direction, owing their coupling to an undeniable throb of the blood. A brother and sister were different, however. Desire for incestuous union was not as sparkling as the desire of a boy for the girl next door. It was born in darkness, out of family secrets and unspeakable knowledge that put pain and distance between the two. Knowing this, neither brother nor sister could make the first move without fear of rejection and disgrace, of staking a lifetime's peace of mind on an irrevocable throw of the dice. The long and short of it was that he and Maureen must and would remain apart.

He was silent at teatime, but Maureen prattled on about the funeral as if nothing had happened in the parlour. When he had tidied up for the night, he told her that he could not bear the house, that he was going to Killage for a drink. He would have preferred to stay at home, but he could not face a long evening alone with her, so he went to Phelan's and found Festus O'Flaherty in a corner of the bar deeply engrossed in a study of his image in the mirror. Kevin wished to talk about cattle and O'Flaherty wished to talk about women, so they talked about women. Festus talked about his favourite train girls, what he called *femmes trouvées* or *cailíní gan iarraidh*, women who come into your life unbidden and leave before they have time to do you an injury, women who have one thing in common—the fact that they never snap back.

Kevin listened in near silence, and as he listened he discovered in himself a new sexual confidence which no amount of bravado from O'Flaherty could obliterate. For the first time he listened to his friend with less than adulatory attention. He had hit upon the truth that in sexual conversation among drinking men a little experience goes a long way.

Maureen was already in bed when he got home, so he sat barefooted in front of the range for half an hour, wondering if O'Flaherty had a sister. Finally, he decided that he would have to go out for a drink every evening for a week, so as to put distance between himself and Maureen and between himself and what had happened in the parlour. Then, after a fortnight or a month, they would be able to resume the innocent round of living they had known before their mother's funeral.

He went to bed at one, and while he lay on his side waiting for sleep, he heard the tread of her bare soles on the linoleum as she felt her way along the corridor to the bathroom. She must have forgotten to close the bathroom door, because he could hear the splashing of her water like that of a mare staling into a gripe. At first he was conscious only of the sound, but gradually he became aware of its duration, and as he wondered when it would stop, he found that he had got an erection for the second time that day. However, it was not one of those erections that distract and torment until relief, manual or orificial, makes bodily ease and sleep a possibility. The feeling that accompanied it was dreamlike in its lack of urgency, so dreamlike that he had fallen asleep before he could hear the dribble of her "strippings" against the side of the bowl. He woke refreshed from what seemed like an interminable slumber to find another body in the bed beside him. He was lying on his side, facing the door, and beside him on the pillow was the dark outline of her head. He listened for a moment to the undeniable urgency of her breathing and decided that there was but one thing to do—pretend to be asleep.

He wasn't wearing pyjamas, only a woollen vest, and she put her hand under it and gently felt the smoothness of his testicles through his barnacled scrotum. She raised her left leg over his thigh until he felt the fire of her vagina burning the eye of his penis, and then he gave a long canine snore and turned on his back, bearing her with him till she was firmly astride him. Still pretending to be asleep, he lay with his arms by his sides while she pulled up his vest so that her breasts were like crushed fruit against the bone and muscle of his chest. Breathing deeply and evenly, and without moving hand or foot, he gave her the freedom of his speculum, allowing her to impale herself to her heart's desire. Her breath was coming in great snorts against his cheek, and as she heaved and plunged, he thought of Henry seeking solace against a wooden post and of Lot lying in a drunken stupor in a cave while his two exemplary daughters did what they could to preserve his seed because there was not a man in the earth to come in unto them after the manner of all the earth. So it was with Maureen.

> And they made their father drink wine that night: and the firstborn went in, and lay with her father; and he perceived not when she lay down, nor when she arose.

At last Maureen arose, and he pulled the bedclothes over his head as if to hide from humankind, but he found himself immersed in the pungency of her sexuality. His bed was no longer a bachelor bed, which pleased him. Like a giant killer in a fairy story she had overcome his invincible virginity, but he could not sleep because of the raw chaos in his soul.

He had sunk so deeply into himself that she was almost upon him before he noticed her. She was making for him between the gaunt trees, Elizabeth Quane, tall and straight, in a heavy coat, muffled against the wind, with a brown ribbon in her combed-back hair. He did not move in recognition; he waited until she had come close enough to talk.

"I didn't recognize you at first. I thought you were a loafing tinker or an unseasonal tourist who had mistaken Slieve Bloom for Macgillicuddy's Reeks."

"I was passing in the car, and I thought I'd come up here for a walk."

She looked at him quizzically, because it was a lame excuse. Midland farmers, he realized, don't spend February days like nature poets under trees. He wondered if she thought that he had come to her wood to relieve himself, and he felt that he would prefer her to think that than that he had come to be alone. He got to his feet because he did not like having to look up into her face.

"I come here because of the river," she said. "I'm interested in music. I sometimes come to listen to the trickle of the water."

He looked into her grey eyes to see if she was making fun of him, but he could see that she was serious, her face composed, her delicate ears pale at the rims.

"When we were growing up, Maureen and I used to come here to swim in the summer. That was before my father sold it."

He wanted to bring the conversation round to a subject

that did not embarrass him, but the thought of Maureen made him distinctly uneasy.

"As soon as Daddy bought it, Murt and I began coming here every day to play in our tree house. It was the only tree we could climb at the time."

They walked along the rutted path with exposed roots like eels petrified in the act of wriggling.

"Do you ever think of Murt?" she asked when they had come to the river.

"I think of him every day."

"You shouldn't feel guilty. It wasn't your fault."

"I miss his conversation most, not for what he said but for the way he said it."

"I miss him too. I'm sorry I never thought of him while I had him—there did not seem to be any need to. He was always there, in and out, coming and going on a tractor. It seemed at the time that those days would last forever. When I think of him now, I see him on a tractor, looking over his shoulder after putting it in reverse."

She was looking down on the brown water of the river flowing smoothly over coarse gravel, and he noticed the vulnerable look in her eyes, as if in her expectation that life would bruise she had not been mistaken. The vulnerability was expressed not merely in her eyes, which looked as if she were in the habit of wearing spectacles and had forgotten to put them on, but also in her nervous smile, which made her mouth look askew. "Askew," he thought, was the wrong word, because it implied imperfection when what he meant was that her face had a look of inwardness and spirituality, achieved rather than bestowed. As he gazed at her, he felt that he'd been seeing her face in a mirror all his life and had now seen it plain for the first time, at once familiar and strange.

"I've had a lovely letter from his girl friend," she continued. "I'm willing to admit that she knew him better than I did."

"I'm afraid I never met her."

"He never mentioned her to me, but now I'm tempted to go to see her."

"I don't think he'd have married her," Kevin said.

"I don't think he'd have married at all."

They walked to the road, she with her head flung back as if it were held by the brown ribbon in her hair.

A rare woman, he thought, but not a comfortable woman. Though she is vulnerable, she is not to be crossed lightly.

"I was sorry to hear that you lost two young bullocks with blackleg," he said when they reached the car.

"I sent for O'Flaherty, but they were dead by the time he arrived."

"He's a good vet, but even a good vet can do little about blackleg."

"I don't think he's a good vet."

"Well, if ever there is anything I can do—"

"Come down for a while tomorrow evening. There are one or two things I want your advice on."

He watched her retreating figure in the rearview mirror as he drove off, and he found himself thinking of sanity and intelligence, of a mind that could penetrate and illumine the fuscous backwaters of life. He was going back to the darkness of Clonglass, of Maureen and Billy Snoddy, while Elizabeth bore with her to Larch Lawn a nimbus of discriminating light.

6

The days lengthened as winter lightened into spring, but he did not find a corresponding lightening in his step. It always roused his sense of wonder to see reddish buds in December preparing so soon after autumn to burst forth greenly in spring, but though it was now the end of February he could discover no vernal hope in his soul. No matter where he went, he could find no more than a few moments' peace, and these only after six or seven pints with O'Flaherty in Phelan's. He tried to prolong these moments by going home for a nightcap with his friend, until Mrs. O'Flaherty came downstairs one night and demanded to know if Festus was a homo or a hetero. If he was the raving hetero he boasted to be, his proper place at two o'clock in the morning was with his wife in bed, not keeping the children awake with drunken guffawing and dirty stories that only showed his hatred of women.

Billy Snoddy's vigilance had changed the timing of Kevin's romps with his sister. Their afternoon couplings had ended. She now came to his bed in the middle of the night, though not every night, nor indeed every week, but irregularly, perhaps once one week, twice the next, and not at all the following week. The lack of regularity in his sexual diet had a disturbing effect on his metabolism, resulting in gripes and flatulence, but knowing not the minute or the hour had at least one advantage. As in practice it meant fewer performances, the pain in his testicles had abated. He was now prepared to accept that it was not a sign of incipient cancer, that it was no more than the ache which any good Irish Catholic would expect to experience after an excess of sexual indulgence. He was sufficiently religious to pray at times for strength to refuse her, but in the darkness of the night he could not find it in himself to deny comfort to a woman in need.

The question of whether Snoddy was dipping his wick in the same oil jar plagued him daily. He kept an eye on them both in the afternoons, but he was too tired to stay awake at night in the hope of surprising them. One day he would tell himself that if Snoddy was servicing his sister she would hardly have to turn to her brother for solace; but the next he would ask himself why she no longer seemed to need the solace of a regular prod. Perhaps he was servicing her but without distinction, so that she had to turn periodically to her prepotent brother for a booster.

He tried to ignore Snoddy but with little success. Though Snoddy could not be faulted in his work during the day, he displayed a moral superiority and axiomatic incisiveness in the evenings which Kevin found difficult to stomach. He had a way of summing up conversations which was enough to daunt any conversationalist, and his summations found force in his unassailable sense of moral ascendancy, of having Kevin and Maureen in his waistcoat pocket.

Kevin knew that he should act. He should tell Snoddy to

pack his bags and scram, or arrange for him to have an accident that would make the packing of bags unnecessary. A fatal accident would be the easier solution because it would be final. The other solution could only end in the spread of gossip about himself and Maureen, which was the last thing he wanted. Though he knew what he wanted to do, he put off doing it from one day to the next. He felt as if he were living in limbo, beyond the flow of grace, condemned forevermore to unease and inaction.

For comfort in his misery, he began visiting Elizabeth Quane twice or three times a week, but he found that his gloom was proof against her conversation. She talked mainly about farming, and when she did not talk about farming, she talked about Murt. He thought that sad. She was an intelligent woman. She could have talked about anything, but clearly she thought that that was not true of him. In her newfound interest in farming she stopped making jokes about PTO shafts and timothy, but she still made fun of him for being much in demand among Macra branches as a speaker on foggage. One cold evening she made him a bowl of pea soup, and when he said that it was good and thick, she replied that she had put lots of foggage in it. In other words she did not see him as a man, did not feel the pull of his flesh and blood.

At the beginning of March, Concepta came with her pampered brood. She was in the habit of coming to see Maureen once a month, and in winter her husband, Monty Kilgallon, often came too, because he liked to tell his staff that he'd spent the afternoon shooting with his brother-in-law. He was a bank manager who suspected now and again that there was more to life than bank balances. He saw the countryside as a playground, and banking as a means of ensuring that the right people played in it. If it had not been for a congenital inability to sit upright on a horse, he would long ago have realized his secret ambition of riding to hounds and being called a fearless horseman by *The Leinster Express*. As a substitute for such fame, he took a sheaf of magazines on shooting and fishing, and to prove to himself that he had read and marked them well he liked to go out with Kevin's gun whenever he came to Clonglass. Kevin detested the sight of him, detested his ostentatious deerstalker, his bright tan shoes, and the carefully planted smell of pipe tobacco that emanated from the pockets of his tweed hacking jacket. Kevin's greatest regret was that once after spending two hours searching the moor for him he pulled him out of a boghole into which he had sunk to the waist.

"Where is Kilgallon?" he asked Concepta as she pulled up in the yard.

"You mean Monty? He's in Dublin on business, so disappointed that he couldn't come. There's nothing he likes better as relaxation from banking than a good conversation about farming."

"He's lucky that he need only talk about it."

Concepta got out of the car and looked at the soles of her shoes in case she had trodden on anything which a bank manager's wife should not tread on.

"Come into the house and change into your old clothes right away, dears. Uncle Kevin's place of work is not as clean as Daddy's," she said to the children in the back of the car.

Three of them emerged dutifully as she spoke, and daintily picked their way across the farmyard. They were dressed to the nines, but to let Kevin and Maureen see that farmyards were not as clean as banks, Concepta always made them take off their finery on arrival and put on the old clothes she brought in a shopping bag. To bring them already dressed for the farm would, of course, have been too simple, too obvious, too lacking in point. All the children had what Concepta and her husband called "quality names." The two girls, aged seven and eight, were called Jocasta and Jacinth; and the boy, who was four, was called Breffny. Concepta was obsessed with the need to preserve the purity of these beautiful names against the despoliation of "common" children who referred to her young as Joc, Jass, and Breff. In a moment of self-revelation she confided to Maureen that if ever God and Monty Kilgallon gave her another child, she would call it Paul or Alice or some other name that could not be savaged by the hoi polloi in their passion for vulgar abbreviation.

"It's a wonder you wouldn't wash that car of yours," she said to Kevin. "There's enough dung on it to manure a square perch."

"Ach, sure it's a great protection against the weather," Kevin said with mock seriousness. "I've never washed a car in my life except when I wanted to sell it. It pays, you know. When I scrape off that crust of cow shit, it will shine like new."

"Take that into the house like a good man," she said, handing him her bulging shopping bag.

"Any sign of you making a move?" she asked as they crossed the yard.

It was her standard question, her way of asking if he were any closer to getting married, and he disliked her for it. He disliked the look of smug superiority that came into her eye as she asked it, almost belying the secret delight he knew her to take in his bachelorhood. He was aware that she thought of Breffny as his heir, the future owner of Clonglass and all the acres that Kevin would acquire for him before he snuffed it. Breffny would not earn his living as a farmer, of course. He would be a landed banker, knowing like his father that land was an asset that neither moth nor fire could destroy.

"What would I be doing with a woman? Amn't I busy enough as it is?"

"You should put yourself in the way of women. You should start going to the dances again. All you do is drink with that good-for-nothing vet from Galway."

"Dance halls are the last place that God created. I'd sooner look for a woman in a cattle mart."

"I have an idea. You should get rid of that evil-smelling weed Snoddy and take on a girl student in his place. Monty knows a farmer this side of Roscrea who's got himself a girl student for a year. You're still in good shape if only you washed and shaved. Get yourself a girl student and you'll be spliced before Christmas."

With ill-concealed relief he left Concepta to Maureen and went out to the workshop to mend the mouldboard of the plough. It was a dark, forbidding afternoon with a threat of rain from the west, and he switched on the light and got out his electric welder. Billy Snoddy came slow-footedly across the yard, and Kevin told him to sharpen the chisels, that he would be needing them tomorrow. After a while the three children came running out of the house in their farm gear. Jocasta and Jacinth told Breffny to stay with Uncle Kevin, and they themselves went off down the lane.

Breffny was a fetching child. He was short, barrel-bodied, and bowlegged, with sandy-red locks that curled cutely about his ears. His plump cheeks were rosy, and when he laughed the gap between his front teeth gave him a look of clownish innocence.

"Come over here, Breff," said Snoddy. "Come over here till I show you the oilstone."

Breffny cared nothing for oilstones, but he was entranced by a box of old bolts that lay unregarded in a corner.

"What's your age?" Snoddy asked.

"Four last birthday. Mammy gave me a black-and-white panda."

"And what will you be when you grow up? A policeman or an engine driver?"

"A bank manager," said Breffny

"Who told you that?"

"Mammy told me in my bedtime story. But she said I was going to be a farmer too."

"How can you be a farmer and a bank manager at the same time?" Snoddy squinted at Kevin.

"Mammy told me that too. She said I'd be a bank manager on weekdays and a farmer on Saturday and Sunday."

"You're a very bright boy and your Mammy is a very bright woman."

"She's not as clever as Daddy. Daddy is better at sums."

"You'll need money to buy a farm, but if you're a bank manager you can lend yourself some," said Snoddy.

"No, I won't. Uncle Kevin is going to leave me his farm when he dies."

"Uncle Kevin is a very healthy man," said Snoddy.

"Mammy says he'll die when he's seventy."

Kevin could listen no longer. He switched on the welder to drown Snoddy's attempt to get at him through Breffny. Snoddy was a coward. He worked indirectly, by hints and darts that found the softest target. Living with him, day in day out, was like standing under the eaves with the cold drip running down your neck. You were constantly aware of him, you could not escape from him, and you had to watch your every word, conceal your thoughts so as not to give the impression that he had a hold on you. As he watched the glare of the arc through the face mask, Kevin regretted not having dropped the sheet of corrugated iron on his neck, and he regretted it all the more because another such opportunity might never arise again.

It was possible, however, to have an accident on the moor with a shotgun on a Sunday afternoon; but the thought of pulling the trigger made him realize that he was not a murderer, at least in the common meaning of the word. No, he would have to devise something more circuitous, something that would not involve him in direct action. He would adapt O'Flaherty's idea of adultery by circumbendibus. Murder by circumbendibus was what was called for, a murder in which he would be an accident manager, the arranger of an act that had been ordained by a higher authority.

He placed the mask on the floor and looked round. Little Breffny had carried the bolts outside and had made a neat pile of them in front of the door. In sudden irritation Kevin caught him by the arm and pulled him roughly away.

"Off with you now, Breffny, and play with Pup in the hay shed."

With tears welling, the boy put a finger in his mouth and ran for the house and his mother.

"He's a bloody nuisance. If he got half a chance, he wouldn't leave a bolt or screw on the premises," Kevin said as he gathered the bolts in both hands.

"Weren't we all like that once? Sure he's only a child," said Billy Snoddy.

Half an hour later Concepta came out to call the children in to tea. Twilight was beginning to gather under the hedges, and Kevin could hear the voices of Jocasta and Jacinth as they came up the lane.

"Breffny, your tea is ready," Concepta called from the gable. "Have you seen Breffny?" she asked the girls.

"He was with Uncle Kevin," Jocasta said.

"Where's Breffny?" she asked Kevin, coming into the workshop.

"He went round behind the hay shed a minute ago."

"Breffny, Breffny," Concepta called. "Don't stand there, Kevin. Look for him," she reproved. "He could have wandered off alone."

Kevin went round behind the hay shed, Concepta ran down the lane, and Billy Snoddy went into Rowan's Field, followed by Jocasta and Jacinth. Kevin was stopped in his tracks by a horrifying thought as Concepta's voice faded behind the trees.

Led by an invisible hand which he half resisted, he went round behind the house and after a moment's hesitation looked into the water tank. Breffny was lying on the bottom in three feet of water, his hair covering his bulbous forehead, his eyes closed and mouth open. He bent down to lift him out, but froze like a pointer in the act. He could not bear to be the finder of the body, to be associated so soon and so directly with another death on the farm. He picked up the broken chair that stood by the tank and put it back in its usual place, by the back door with a bucket on top of it. Then he went into the house and asked Maureen if she had seen Breffny. Concepta came up the lane and went round behind the house. Kevin, making for the cow houses, spun round as her horrified shriek gripped at his throat.

"What's wrong?" he asked as he ran to her.

"Dead, dead. Drowned in your bloody tank," she wailed as she hugged the dripping body to her breast.

Tears ran into her mouth, and the water from Breffny's clothes ran down the front of her dress, so that she looked as if she had just risen from the river.

"There may be some life left in him," Kevin said, thinking that Breffny in her arms looked bigger than he did alive.

"Go away, you clumsy stookaun. The water tank was always covered when we were children. Oh, no, my lovely boy."

Concepta went into the house, and Kevin told Snoddy to fodder the cattle, that he was going to drive his sister home.

"You're jinxed," Snoddy said. "The black ox has trod

94

on your foot, on your two feet. It's the second death in this yard inside two months. The wages of sin is no longer death to the sinner but death to every innocent man and child he knows. I had better look out."

Kevin walked off without answering. He felt beaten into dizziness and he walked as if the power of movement was ebbing from his legs. He did not want to go into the house for fear of what Maureen might look or say, so he shuffled round the back and peered down into the tank through the gathering dusk.

"How did he climb up the side?" Snoddy asked from behind. "It's at least three feet high without either hand- or foothold."

"I have no idea," Kevin said.

"Have you thought that the supernatural could have lent a hand?"

"What are you talking about?"

"You know what I'm talking about," said Snoddy, turning on his heel to go.

Maureen led Concepta out of the house, Concepta carrying the body in a blanket, babbling hysterically about the boy and his father.

"I wouldn't mind . . . oh, my lovely boy . . . but Monty always told me not to take the children here . . . my only boy."

Kevin opened the boot of the Mercedes but she shouted witheringly, "No, no, no, you insensitive eejit, I'll nurse him on my knee."

He told the two girls to get in beside him. Concepta sat with Maureen in the back, hugging Breffny to her breast and crooning vacantly into his unhearing ear.

Jocasta and Jacinth held hands as if they could not grasp that they would never play with Breffny again. Maureen said nothing, and Kevin drove without noticing the traffic, reexperiencing the day the tree fell on Murt Quane. Now and again he shivered as if the cold water that had folded over Breffny had seeped through the marrow of his bones, and now and again he would think to himself, First men, then cattle.

He and Maureen stayed at the wake until after midnight, and the following day he went to the funeral and hung uneasily on the edge of the knot of mourners in the graveyard. Though neither Monty Kilgallon nor anyone except Concepta had breathed a hint of reproach, he felt as if his life had darkened beyond possibility of light, and he was surprised when an A.I. man whom he had not seen for over a year shook his hand in friendly recognition.

After taking Maureen home, he drove straight to Larch Lawn, not knowing why but vaguely suspecting that he must tell Elizabeth his version of events. He was pleased, therefore, when she took both his hands and held them for what seemed like a full minute.

"You poor fellow," she whispered. "First Murt, now this. But don't blame yourself. Bad luck, like good luck, comes in runs, my father used to say. I hope you've come to the end of yours."

It was the first time she had talked to him about anything except her brother and the farm, and he was pleased, because in a small way it eased the dry grinding of his thoughts.

7

In the days after the drowning, Kevin thought of himself as an outwardly sound apple whose core had been eaten by the grub of the codling moth. To a casual observer, he looked as he had always looked, but within him was a tearing and a gnawing, an unceasing awareness that he was the quarry and that he was being stalked by no less a hunter than the gentleman on the pale horse. He had once read in a schoolbook that Sleep is Death's brother, but more terrifying was the knowledge that Sex is Death's sister. It did not require much imagination to see that by losing himself in such a sister he was giving fortune an irrecoverable hostage. He asked himself why he believed in such fairy tales, but all he could reply was that he believed. The man on the pale horse had ridden off with Murt and then with Breffny. Who was next? From time to time he would tell himself that he was being fanciful, that both of them died in accidents that had nothing to do with his sin, but his thoughts always returned to the rider and the horse whose hooves do not ring on the road to warn of his approach.

One day, as he was returning from the mill with a load of sawdust for bedding, it occurred to him that God, not Death, was the problem, God who callously employed Death as his chela, as one of the many instruments of terror from his chamber of horrors. He knew nothing of God except what the priests and his own imagination told him, and for the first time in his life he asked himself what kind of god he believed in. He rejected one image after another until he thought of a solitary white cloud in a clear blue sky. He remembered seeing it on the moor on a summer day as he lay on his back eating frochans and listening to a lark filling the silence with such heart that the very air burgeoned with merriment and song. His eye followed the white cloud as an airplane overtook it. The airplane vanished, and after a minute or two reappeared on the other side. He realized now that what he had seen was God in one of his many manifestations. To one man he was a nightingale singing, to another a radiant sunrise, and to yet another a rising wave of the sea, but to Kevin Hurley he would now be a White Cloud in a Blue Sky. He could embrace you as the cloud embraced the airplane, but you could not embrace him. He could envelop you as a sea mist might envelop a lost ship, but you could never use your science to put him in a glass jar, hermetically sealed to impress your friends at a harvest supper.

He was not a provident god who had numbered the very hairs on your head and took a personal interest in the fall of a sparrow, but a remote and callous deity whose breath was cold as mountain mist in January, who made the earth as a clockmaker might make a clock and then withdrew into a remote corner of the universe to enjoy the ticking and at the end the final croak. Could such an impersonal and inhuman deity stoop to wreak vengeance on the wicked who were surely beneath his contempt? Would he not say, "I have made them wicked. I have wound up the clock, and now I shall listen to the ticking, however tiresome, until the spring runs down a billion or more years from now?" For a moment Kevin also listened, but he heard no answer in his heart. He knew, however, that it was not in his nature to be an atheist. If he did not believe in the White Cloud, he would have to believe in the Vacuum where it used to be—an even more terrifying option. He was stuck with himself as he was. He would have to accept the burden of his guilt and try to find the strength to cleanse himself, not merely because of White Cloud but to appease the ache of his own nature.

He tried to stay away from Maureen, to talk to her only in the presence of Billy Snoddy, but she would come to his room in the middle of the night and lie against his belly, breathing on his eyelids until he was moved to caress her.

"We must stop this," he said one night after he had assuaged the ache that long habit and her robust imagination provoked.

"Why?"

"Because it's not right."

"Don't turn crawthumper on me now. I know how religious you are! You only go to confession and Communion once a year, just to do your Easter Duty, and then you're afraid to go to Monsignor McGladdery. You go all the way to Roscrea to confess to the monks, God help us."

"It's got nothing to do with clergy. It's against the current of my own nature."

"If it is, you were a long time finding out. We've done it so often now that it's second nature. If you were to stop, who knows if I could? Do you really want me to turn to Billy Snoddy?"

"You've played flame to his candle once before."

"Only once, and it was no good. We were made for

each other, you and me. We fit like hand and glove. When you move in me, it's like an earthquake, but Billy Snoddy spent his handful of coppers at the first standin'—I came against dead mutton."

"I prefer beef," he said without thinking.

"Beef with the cut of mustard. That's what it's all about." She laughed, and he could not help warming to the homeliness of her humour.

"Do you think of me during the day?" she asked.

"I'm a man, not a woman. I'm too busy to think about sex."

"I think about you, and when I go out to the yard I sometimes stand and watch Henry. I think you're better than Henry, even though you're not as heavy."

"What has weight got to do with it?"

"I like to move against the full brunt of a man. Billy Snoddy was too careful. He did it on his knees and elbows, but I couldn't help laughing when it occurred to me that the cottager was more of a gentleman than the farmer who employed him."

After that conversation, it was difficult to deny her solace. He did not wish her to turn to Snoddy, and besides, the directness of her humour had fired his imagination. He realized that here was a woman whom only a gifted man could satisfy, that compared with her, other women were so lacking in vigour that a thundering twankydillo would turn them into nervous wrecks; and he realized too that because of her he led two lives, his own life on the farm and an idealized life in her lively imagination which conferred on him a kind of immortality. He was grateful to her for mentioning Henry, because now he often thought of Henry during the act, which added the force of fantasy to the grossness of sexual pleasure. At the back of his mind, however, was the thought that all pleasure was transient, that one day the blood would cool, that he might enjoy the peace of an evening sun.

In the meantime he ate his meals in silence while the Abominable Ruminant sat opposite, impassive as a buddha, counting the spoonfuls of mustard as they came out of the pot.

"Do you believe in a run of bad luck?" he asked Kevin as he topped up the battery of the heavy tractor.

"I believe in bad luck at cards and the races."

"You can have bad luck with cattle too, and you can have bad luck with women—if you're weak enough to love a woman. Thank your lucky stars that so far your farming luck has held."

Kevin resented the obliquity of Snoddy's probing, because it seemed to say that what Snoddy knew was too grievous to be expressed directly. He longed to take the galoot by the scruff of the neck and rub his nose in his own dung as he would have done to a dog that refused to respond to house training. But he always stayed his hand in tacit acknowledgement of the havoc that Snoddy could wreak on him.

The evenings were the most trying times. Maureen would sit knitting before the television while Snoddy reread the local newspaper and toasted the soles of his stockinged feet before the range and the grandfather clock hoarsely marked the slowness of the hours. At first he took to going outside and standing in one of the cow houses, drawing comfort from the innocence of animal breathing and the occasional cough from a cud-chewing bullock. Then he found that all rumination reminded him of the Abominable Ruminant, and he would jump into the car and drive recklessly to Killage for a drink. On these nights he avoided Phelan's, because he never went there without a wash, a shave, and a change of socks and shoes. Instead he went from pub to pub, drinking a pint in each until it was time to head for home. He would gaze at the television in the corner of the bar, not caring about the picture but thinking about Maureen turning the heel of a sock for him, fighting the impulse to drive home at once and catch the Ruminant covering her on knees and elbows.

On Mondays and Fridays he washed and shaved and drove to Larch Lawn to see Elizabeth. She had shown herself to be a woman of parts. Four months ago farming talk for her was something to be scoffed at; now she could discuss dry stock and tillage for two hours without once putting a foot wrong. She had begun reading *The Farmers' Journal,* and already she knew enough to keep the foreman and the farmhands on their toes. At first he went to see her to give encouragement and advice, but soon he saw that she was in need of neither. She no longer asked questions; she just told him what had happened on the farm in the last few days and gave at least two good reasons for each of her decisions.

In Kevin's eyes the death of Breffny had achieved one good: it made Elizabeth see him as a man. It made her feel for him, at least for a time, and her sympathy gave him a strange, unexpected pleasure, like a pervasive warmth in the stomach after neat whiskey on a cold night. He would sit at the kitchen table drinking the glass of ale she had placed before him while she told him about a new topic she had discovered—what had happened at school that day. At other times he would watch her move about the kitchen like a water bird on long, perfect legs, her heels sharply clacking on the tiles, making a coldly impersonal sound that might inspire fear in unruly infants. She always wore a tight dark skirt with a slit that accentuated the roundness of her little bottom, and a white blouse that made him wonder if the bra inside it was empty or half full. Her brown hair was straight, drawn back tightly over her ears in a ponytail, which she secured with a ribbon that matched the colour of her skirt, and as she talked she would run her long fingers over her temples, smoothing hair that was already faultless in its smoothness.

The overall effect of her body was one of icy elegance, which was somehow belied by her pallid face, her weakest feature. She had a sharp, slightly squarish jaw, square front teeth which her upper lip did not quite cover, and greyish eyes that stared more often than they smiled. Her voice, however, was unforgettable. It pursued him into the fields, ringing in his ear in moments of silence, nudging him into surprised remembrance. Unlike women in fur coats he had seen in Phelan's, she did not speak as if she were afraid the words would melt in her mouth; she intoned them through her high, thin nose like a lady archbishop with a heavy cold reading an admonitory epistle from St. Paul.

One evening as she let him in, she told him that she had been practising on the piano. She gave him a drink and put him sitting by the bright little turf fire in the parlour while she played with her back to him, rocking gently on the stool, one ear inclined to the keyboard as if the very act of listening could elicit perfect music. He sat awkwardly, with the firelight on his face and the glass on the arm of his chair, wondering what on earth he would say to her when the piece was over. He only knew about fiddle and accordion music, and this could not be compared with any sound he had heard from either of those estimable instruments. Luckily, when she finished, she closed the piano and said something about the hard weather, a remark to which he responded as if it were manna from heaven.

That was the first of many evenings in the parlour while she played things she called sonatas as if she had forgotten his very existence. He now realized that the piano was her instrument of defence. She was not an ingenious conversationalist. They had exhausted such obvious topics as her brother, the farm, and the school, and now she was making him listen in silence to the only conversation that came naturally to her. She put him in mind of the young widow Festus once courted in Abbeyleix. Whenever Festus put his hand up her skirt, she would cry "Jesus, Mary, and Joseph!" and reach for the pack of cards on the mantelpiece. "But they're the Devil's prayer book," Festus would say to her as he inspected the hand she had dealt him, and she would invariably reply that "a prayer book is a prayer book, be it God's or the Devil's." Kevin would have preferred cards to music, because they would have encouraged a kind of conversation he could understand, but Elizabeth was not the widow from Abbeyleix, nor he himself Festus O'Flaherty.

Sometimes he asked himself why she encouraged him in his visits. Did she really enjoy his slow talk or was she using him as a shield against loneliness while she waited for a doctor or a vet? She was an unusual girl; she rarely went places where she might attract the attention of eligible bachelors. For all her education, perhaps she was a realist who did not consider it beneath her to turn to the one man who had beaten a path to her door. Or perhaps she was a woman who sought simplicity in men, who would turn her back on the moral uncertainties and sophistication to which she herself was prone.

Whatever the answer, he realized all too keenly that he could easily make an ass of himself. Festus had already begun to make jokes about his "floozie," and what Festus said today the neighbours would say tomorrow. Though he was reluctant to be swayed by country gossips, he was determined not to repeat the mistake of Robert John Carroll, who lived a life of exemplary devotion to a widow and died a virgin for his pains. Robert John fell irretrievably in love with her as he saw her tears stain the wood of her husband's coffin. For twenty years he went to see her every evening, neglecting his own farm to help on hers. After ten years without overt progress the neighbours said that he was a right eejit. Then, as the widow's daughter reached puberty, they said that he was no daw, that he had more than one iron in the fire, or more than one fire for his iron. But when the daughter married a younger man and Robert John got the cold shoulder because his help was no longer needed on the farm, they said that they had foreseen the ending from the start, that there was no fool like a widow's fool. Kevin thought of Robert John growing old alone, watching the widow from a distance at Sunday Mass while she made novenas for her long-dead husband, and he told himself that Elizabeth was a virgin, not a widow.

Spring came slowly. The buds burst on the boughs, on one tree today and on another tomorrow, but he felt no answering burgeoning in his blood, unusual in a man whose life had always reflected the changing rhythm of the seasons. He did not even look forward to the farmer's first day of spring, the day he'd drive the cattle out to grass once more. He felt that he was trapped in an iron cage to which only Elizabeth had the key. Moreover, he felt defiled by his proximity to Billy Snoddy. He felt that he must cleanse himself—of Snoddy, of Maureen, of the daily expectation of cataclysmic retribution. That he would achieve by an act of courage requiring a moral effort and personal upheaval beyond any he had hitherto experienced. In short he would marry Elizabeth. The thought of marriage to her filled him with a sense of uncertainty and inadequacy. Marriage, he had learnt from O'Flaherty, was an act of such irrationality that only a man who was head over heels in love could enter into it without heart-searching trepidation. As he himself was far from being in love, he could feel in his bones the force of the manly reluctance which he must now overcome.

The marriage, however, was worth making because of the good that would flow from it. As a married man living in harmony with a satisfied wife, he would be less vulnerable to any gossip that Snoddy might broadcast about himself and Maureen. In fact, once married, he would tell Snoddy to take a long walk on a short pier. And moreover, he could not forget that as Elizabeth's husband, he would be a more substantial man with weightier opinions because of the prospering farm that went with her.

Though he would not marry her merely for her farm, he could not ask for her hand without acknowledging that there was no hunger like land hunger. Unlike sexual hunger, land hunger was never satisfied. You could inherit land, you could buy it, or you could marry into it, but still you craved for more. Ye shall eat the fat of the land, the priests said. And if you went to the bank for a loan, the bank manager would ask how many acres you had to your name. He would give a well-heeled farmer a loan of £50,000 but he would refuse to lend a cottager £500 towards the price of a secondhand car. Everyone respected land and also the men with a stake in it. Even Billy Snoddy, a cynic without a rood to build a house on, was in the habit of saying, "Your best friend is your farm" or "Land, like money, talks and talks." But land for Kevin meant more than money. It was a deeply sensuous experience. It sprang under your boot as you walked; it almost hugged you as you stretched on it in summer; it yielded like a woman before the coulter; and in the end it received you as if you were its own. As he felt the pull of the land in his bone marrow, he admitted that marriage to Elizabeth required less moral courage than he had at first envisaged. And as he thought of her milch cows walking sluggishly home in the evening, heavy with milk, their hind legs chafing the blue veins of their elders (what she called udders), he experienced an indescribable sense of comfort, as if he had already laid his head upon her breasts.

But he had not laid his head upon her breasts; he had not even laid a hand on her knee. At the rate he was progressing, he would take a lifetime to get within kissing range, and how could he ask her to marry him without first caressing her? He pondered this conundrum for four days, and on the morning of the fifth the answer came to him. He would surprise her. He would propose first and kiss later.

He waited until the black buds of the ash trees had burst on the bough, then he entered her parlour and said to her across the room, "Elizabeth, will you marry me?"

"I wondered when you were going to ask me that," she replied.

"You already know the answer, then?"

"No, I don't. I never cross a bridge until I've come to it."

"You've come to it now."

"Today is Monday. I'll tell you on Friday."

"I'll let you think in peace then," he said and left the room.

On Friday she told him that she would marry him in Killage parish church on May nineteenth, on the feast of St. Prudentiana, Virgin, daughter of a Roman senator. The piano was between them when she said it, and he walked round it to embrace her. She caught his clumsy hands and squeezed them but turned away when he tried to kiss her.

"You were sufficiently original to propose without once kissing me. Now I shall be sufficiently original to deny you a kiss till we're married."

"It's more odd than original."

"No, it isn't. We'll enjoy ourselves all the more when we've got a licence."

"Is it because you don't wish me to touch you?"

"You mustn't ask me questions, Kevin. You must take me as I am or not at all."

As he drove home, a half moon was riding over the Grove. He stopped the car and walked into the darkness under the trees, crossing little clearings of pale light where her father had cut some of the larches for fencing. He sat on a log and rested his back against a tree trunk, listening to the flutterings of nervous wood pigeons in the branches. He could not see the moon from where he sat, but her watery light had washed the little clearing at his feet, giving the shadows of twigs, sticks, and young ferns the quality of exaggeration. The same moon was looking down on every hedge and field, on every road and lane in the midlands, all of them bathed in the same levelling light, dim and shadowy so that outlines merged, so that you could not say where one object ended and another began. In his parlour he knew that at this moment her light was picking out the transoms of the windows but not the mullions, that the white-painted horizontal bars would look as if they'd been heaped with snow, that the pattern of the windowpanes would lie obliquely across the bare tabletop, and that Maureen and Snoddy in the kitchen would be utterly unaware of it. He closed his eyes to listen to the night sounds, but all he could hear was the measured pessimism of his own voice within him.

I'm leaving the sunlight for the moonlight, it said. For a long time the sunlight has been dim, but on the darkest day it is clearer than the brightest night.

"I'm getting married, Daddy," he said the following day as he turned his father on his left side, but his father did not seem to hear.

"Have you seen Donie Dunne today? Is he still sitting outside the house?" he asked.

"Didn't I tell you the other day he died of constipation."

"Donie Dunne will never die. He's like me. He will live forever. There comes a time in a man's life when all he can do is breathe and stay lukewarm in bed, when it takes as much energy to die as to live. Donie Dunne and myself have reached that stage."

His father crossed his hands over the bedclothes and sniffled. "He always gave off a strange smell, did Donie," he said. "I remember your mother, God rest her, saying it after he came here to a threshing."

"He's now giving off gases in Killage churchyard."

"I wonder if he eats goody."

"Not unless the Devil cooks it."

"Have you heard the latest about Dev?"

"He didn't kill Michael Collins after all."

"No, he's going to introduce the British Landrace to Ireland, but he's going to call it the Swedish Landrace. No other breed of pig will be allowed in Ireland's four green fields."

"But the Landrace is Swedish," Kevin said.

"No, it's British, at least as British as Dev is Irish. The bloody Spaniard, he'll wreck us and fuck us in his black overcoat before he releases his death grip on the country."

Kevin felt confused. Since his mother's death three years ago, his father's mind had been anchored in the 1930s, but now he was going on about the British Landrace, which wasn't introduced into England until after the war. He looked at the withered face dotted with the brown and black spots of old age, and he wondered what macabre phantoms were fleeing through his addled imagination. Was this to be the final dissolution, a concourse of pigs and republicans presided over by Eamon De Valera?

"I'm getting married, Daddy," he said again.

"If I live till you get married, I'll live to be as old as Methuselah."

"What else do you want before I go?"

"I want you to stop talking about that bloody Spaniard for a start. Never mention his name to me again."

"But I thought you liked to talk about him."

"He's dead and never saw my age."

"If you want to talk about him, you're welcome. He froze this country into a mould that won't be broken for three generations."

"Why do you humour me?"

"How?"

"Talking like this. You know that Dev is dead, that you sold the mare, that the Grove is Quane's. You must be sick to death of seeing me here."

"I like to hear what you have to say," he lied in order to soothe.

"You think the words of the half-dead have more pith in them than the words of the half-alive."

"Maybe."

"I'd swap places with you if I could. I would rather be half alive than half dead. When are you going to throw your leg on a woman?"

"I'm marrying Elizabeth Quane on the nineteenth of May. The Grove will be ours again, as if we'd never lost it."

"That's what the bachelor life does to you, makes you soft in the head. Next you'll be telling me that Dev is still eating goody in the Vice-Regal Lodge. He died, I tell you, on the twenty-ninth of August, 1975, and they wrote 'Aged Ninety-two' on his coffin."

His father closed his eyes and allowed his chin to droop on his chest. Kevin closed the bedroom door and went downstairs with a sense of besiegement.

Snoddy was in the yard and Maureen in the kitchen making bread.

"I'm marrying Elizabeth Quane," he said, sitting down behind a newspaper.

"You're what?"

"On the nineteenth of May in Killage. You're the first I've invited to the wedding."

"Thank you very much."

"What else have you got to say?"

"You'll live to rue it. She's a cold fish and a cold lady. Gentleman John, if he ever gets that far, will feel the difference."

"She's a landed woman."

"She's landed you, all right, and you haven't the sense to ask yourself why."

"She just likes me gimp, said it herself. There are ladies who get sick of cake. They get hungry for soda bread."

"You know nothing about her. She's fierce and fanatical. You can tell by the straightness of her back and the way she looks down her nose as she walks."

"That's because she's shortsighted from reading books."

"She's read you like a book, you oul' eejit, and she'll bleed you dry as a keck, wait and see. Where are you going to live, the two of you?"

"Here, where else?"

"With me and Billy Snoddy. She won't like that."

"Billy Snoddy will go as soon as you drop your burden."

"I'm not dropping anything." She laughed.

"What?"

"I went to Dr. Blizzard a few weeks ago with a pain in the back as an excuse, and he told me that I'd reached the menopause."

"And what in God's name is that?"

"The change of life. It came to me earlier than most women."

"So it was cloudburst after all—after all I've been through because of you."

111

"Who's going to be the woman of the house when she comes?"

"My wife, who else?"

"Well, I'm not taking any orders from any Quane."

"I'll change her name to Hurley to make it easier," he said, getting up to go.

"I hear you're marrying into land," Billy Snoddy told him that evening.

"All you need to know is that I'm marrying."

"It won't make any difference between you and me. You'll need a farmhand now more than ever, with two women to look after instead of one."

Kevin walked away in case he should lose his temper, telling himself that Snoddy was in for a surprise, He went down to Larch Lawn after nightfall and found Elizabeth wallpapering her bedroom, or "our bedroom" as she called it.

"But we'll be living in Clonglass," he said.

"I want to live here. The house is bigger and more modern, and we'll have it all to ourselves."

They had a long but amicable argument, and finally she promised to come to see Clonglass next day. She came "like visiting royalty," as Maureen put it, and drank one cup of tea with himself and his sister while Billy Snoddy was, by no means accidentally, on an errand in town. Then she went away as suddenly as she had arrived, and the kitchen seemed empty of everything but her perfume for half an hour. Two days later she handed him a list of changes he must make if she was to join him at Clonglass. She demanded a new toilet and bathroom with a bidet, central heating in all the rooms, a music room, a flower garden for herself, and a new double bed which she had seen advertised in a glossy magazine. He told her that he could not do everything at once but that he would make a start on the bathroom and toilet with the bidet right away. He had never heard of a bidet before, which did not make his task any easier, but he knew that if it had anything to do with sex, Festus O'Flaherty would be only too pleased to enlighten him.

He asked Festus to be his best man, and Festus promised to be on his best behaviour on the day, though he confided that he would much prefer to goose the bride than kiss her. As the nineteenth of May fell on a Saturday, they met on Friday for a little celebration, for what Festus called a "two-stag party."

"It's your last night free," he said as he proposed a toast. "When a man marries, he goes to stud. The night and its dreams are no longer his own."

Festus was more excited than Kevin. He genuinely saw his friend as a comrade-in-arms who had finally bitten the dust, and he convinced him that he should mark the occasion by scorning pints and celebrating in neat malt whiskey. Over the first six doubles they talked seriously about cattle, and then suddenly they found themselves in serious conversation about women.

"Consider yourself lucky," Festus said. "You're getting married with both eyes open. At forty you're no longer twenty, no longer at an age when you marvel at the existence of women. You've seen them on bad days as well as good, in curlers as well as evening dress. You've lived with them and without them; you've glimpsed both sides of the coin. The man who gets married at twenty thinks he knows his woman, especially if she's been confident enough in her charms to allow him to anticipate marriage, and most young women are overconfident these days. But the truth is that he knows nothing about her that matters. He may know her two breasts and seven orifices, he may be intoxicated by the shared secrets of the flesh, but he knows nothing of the chrysalis in her heart containing the monster that will emerge in her middle age. The change that overtakes a married woman is more diabolical than any change wrought by time. The running of the house, the luxury of spending without having to get, the moulding of children, the realization that at last she has a habitation and a name—all these things give her ideas above her station, sometimes above her husband's station. What I am saying at such length, dear Kevin, is that when a man marries he domesticates a tigress."

"Why a tigress?"

"A carnivore who will smile as she consumes him."

"I've seen women who sweeten everyone they talk to."

"Are you drunk enough to hear the truth?"

"I am sober enough to recognize it."

"The truth about Elizabeth?"

"Tell it if you can."

"You should watch her. She's got a classical face, clear-cut features that mirror an icy heart. She has a will that can only be conquered by snaffle and curb, the two things that the modern woman most stridently rejects."

Festus was more than tipsy. He had reached the stage of drunkenness when he would order two double whiskeys and drink his own while the barman was still pouring Kevin's. He was in one of his conspiratorial moods in which he continually looked over his shoulder before speaking and gripped Kevin's forearm as he whispered in his ear.

"What a man needs in a wife is moral not physical beauty," he continued. "You need a warm heart more than a pretty nose. Now, Elizabeth has physical beauty, but has she the sweetness of nature to match it? I think she's a filly, and there you have my sympathy."

"What do you mean?"

"Womankind can be divided into two classes: fillies and heifers. Fillies are slender, small-breasted, quick-footed, intelligent, and excitable. That's your Lizzie. Heifers are heavy and slow, with udders for breasts and a tendency to sleep.

114

Most men would prefer to be seen out with a filly in the evening, but they'd prefer to spend the night with a heifer. Heifers make the truest and trustiest bedfellows. They eat a lot, think little, and are content with only scant attention."

"If that's your view of women, why do you pursue them?" Kevin asked.

"I pursue them for the same reason a cat will pursue a mouse. You've often seen cats that will kill mice and never eat them. Well, I'm the same with women. My pleasure is in the chase, in bringing the quarry to bay, not in the consumption. Once a woman drops her knickers I lose all interest, though I must admit that now and again curiosity overcomes me, the desire to see if she's musical, if she has a sense of rhythm on the short strokes. But once I've found out, I look round for the next. I've had a lot of women in the last five years, not one of them twice."

"Come on now, Festus, tell the truth. What about the widow from Clonaslew?"

"She's the exception that proves the rule. I keep going back because she's an eminently penetrable lady, but even she has her faults. If I didn't keep her on such a tight rein, she'd be telling me within a week that until I met her I didn't know the cure for white scour in calves."

At closing time Festus invited Kevin back for what he called "a last drink single." He did not want another drink, and neither did he want to disturb Mrs. O'Flaherty, but when Festus said that they would have only one drink and that they would have it in the garage he agreed. O'Flaherty opened the garage doors, drove in, and closed them again. Kevin got into the front beside him while he opened a half-bottle of Scotch which he had secreted in the glove compartment.

"We've had our last night out together," he said after a while.

"Nonsense. I'll still come to Phelan's on Saturday's."

"Brave words, Kevin, but we'll see."

"You're drunk, Festus. You drink too much, enough to ruin the health of a stronger man."

"I drink no more than I need. My choice is not between a ripe old age and cirrhosis of the liver at fifty, but between the madhouse at forty and cirrhosis at fifty. Dear God, give me cirrhosis before madness."

"Why madness?"

"It's a constant battle with the tigress. I stay with her only because of the children. Surely, you must know that only a very unhappy man would waste his life on women, monsters in fancy dress. There's nothing I'd like better than to spend an evening with a book at my own fireside, but I can't. One day you may see what I mean, but for your own sake I hope you never do."

As he talked, O'Flaherty started the car and left the engine running. He was muttering into his chest, his head bent over the padded steering wheel, and in the effort to understand him Kevin failed to notice the rising smell of the exhaust fumes.

"Christ!" he said when they finally made him cough. He jumped out of the car and opened the garage doors.

"You bloody madman, you could have poisoned us both."

"'Bridegroom and Best Man Found Dead in Car. Suicide Pact Suspected.'" O'Flaherty laughed, but there was more bitterness than mirth in his voice.

"See you at the chapel at eleven. And don't be late," Kevin said, walking away.

He drove home with exaggerated care, his eyes fixed on the centre of the road, only half aware of the hedge on each side rushing to meet him and the delicate smell of hawthorn blossom coming through the window. At each crossroads without a give-way sign he stopped, switched off the lights and waited to see if another car was coming. Then he nosed slowly forward, telling himself that Festus knew nothing about women.

When he reached home, he tiptoed up the stairs and lay over the bedclothes without undressing. The room was spinning like a top, and he felt that the foot of the bed was higher than the head one minute and lower the next. He disliked whiskey. As long as he lived he would never taste another drop of it. But the daemons at the bedside laughed in his ear and told him that tomorrow was the day of wrath and tonight a night of infernal temptation.

Will you be able to serve two women? they jeered. Easier to serve God and Mammon. Will you be able to please Elizabeth because your trousers never bulged in her parlour? She is just the kind of girl you might fail with, and if you do, will the marriage be null and void? "Annulment of Farmer's Marriage on Grounds of Impotence." Headlines in *The Leinster Express*. Sniggers at Macra meetings. Double-edged jokes about foggage.

Another daemon opened his bedroom door and touched his face with her forefinger, tracing on his cheek the secret sign she normally traced on his buttocks. She shook him by the shoulder, but he pretended to be fast asleep.

"Kevin, it's Maureen," she said, but he groaned wearily and buried his head deeper in the pillow.

She gripped him between the legs and shook him again, but all his feeling had dissolved, and she went away as silently as she had come. The last thing he heard before sleep was the hoot of an owl and the splash of her water against the side of the bowl.

It was six when he woke. He had a scalp-rending headache which he half attributed to the dream that tormented him in the night. As he dreamt, he felt certain that he had

117

experienced it all many times before, but now he knew that it was a new dream, a dream for a new and different life.

Twelve of his heifers calved together in the cow house and he lay over the bedclothes watching them on closed-circuit television, watching them lick their calves while their afterbirths hung in wads that reached to their hocks. He went out and shook salt and pepper on their cleanings and then untied them one after the other. They followed him out into the yard and walked round him in a circle, each cow eating the dangling afterbirth of the one that went before. Outside the circle trying to get in was Elizabeth dressed in an A.I. man's smock, but all he could do was wave to her and wait till the cows had finished their extraordinary meal.

The dream was now a cloud in his mind; he could not say if the cows were Herefords or Friesians or if they had a good show of milk. And he could not say what it meant, though as he dreamt it he had marvelled at its simple inevitability. Then he recalled that he was to be married in Killage parish church at eleven, and the sobering thought banished all oneirocriticism from his mind.

He got up before Snoddy and went out to the cow house while he waited for the kettle to boil. One of his heifers, the one he called Rotten Socks, had unexpectedly come round. Henry had served her with his customary gusto last time, but the slight show of blood behind told him that she had not proved. He would release His Rampancy after breakfast and watch his last service as a single man. In his early bachelor days he often wondered about the care he took of his heifers, how he rarely missed the signs of heat, and how he would give Henry a helping hand if in his eagerness he sought the upper chamber. Now he would be married like any other man, and if he took pleasure in Henry's service, he would not feel guilty because he himself lacked a licence.

He ate a plate of beef and cold baked beans for breakfast with a wedge of soda bread and three cups of tea.

"I suppose we should eat lightly," Billy Snoddy said. "We'll be having a good breakfast in Phelan's after you're spliced."

"Dinner," Kevin said.

"I'll bet Elizabeth Hurley née Quane will call it breakfast."

"You can call it supper if you like. It will still be my dinner, because I'm having my breakfast now."

"It must be a great feeling getting the licence," Snoddy said.

"The only difference is that you take a greater interest than usual in the weather."

"I would expect you to feel a little flutter, not in your stomach but in your trousers, maybe."

"That reminds me," Kevin said. "Rotten Socks is bulling. We'll have to see that she gets her due after breakfast."

When Henry had done his duty, Kevin had a bath, but he still did not put on his wedding garment, a three-piece suit he had bought four years ago and had never worn. He was going to wear the waistcoat today so that he could sport his grandfather's gold watch, which had not ticked in living memory. He went out to the yard and leant over the gate, wondering if his cows would seem different tomorrow and thinking about the Connemara bridegroom who, according to Festus, said, "Stand back, boys, till I make my last piss single."

At ten o'clock Maureen called him and told him to get ready. She had polished his Sunday shoes and laid out his suit on the bed. It was a tight fit. The trousers needed no belt and the jacket barely buttoned, but as he studied his handsome face in the mirror, he told himself that there would be more

119

ill-fitting suits at his wedding. When they were about to leave, Maureen gave him a thermos flask of whiskey-laced tea to take up to his father. The old man was lying on his back, his eyes closed and mouth open, and suddenly Kevin knew without touching him that he was dead. All that seemed left in the bed was the narrow bird's head with its fringe of white hair, the rest of him so wasted that his form was barely discernible under the clothes. His forehead was cold. He must have died soon after breakfast. Now De Valera could sleep in peace, because there was no one left who remembered with such passion the rigour of his oratory and the satanic sweep of his black overcoat. He straightened his father's legs, closed his mouth, and tucked the bedclothes under his chin so that the jaw would not drop again.

He opened the window and breathed the first fresh air that had entered the room in years. Beyond was the Red Gate, a hawthorn hedge with white blossom, and black-and-white Friesian calves grazing with angular rumps. It was a minutely private world, a world in which the world could forget you, and his father had left it more or less as he found it. He had planted a hedge here and dug a drain there. He had contributed a story or two to local folklore which would survive him by a decade, and he had lost four fields and a patch of woodland which would be more than recovered by his son. For fifty years he had ploughed and harrowed, sown and harvested, but still the land had retained its secret. The land was greater than the landowner. Though it might yield to the thrust of his coulter and respond to his husbandry, it lived a life of its own which gave it the last word and the last laugh.

The calves took off down the field with stiff tails. He remembered his boyhood and the boorish tyranny of his father. He remembered the Grove and how his father had to sell it after a bad year, while Elizabeth's father had had a good enough year to buy it. His father had been an encumbrance, a withered thistle that could still prick long after the sap had dried in it. He had been contrary in his old age. He had refused to make over the farm to his son, but now Kevin would have the property administered and the brown official envelopes that came a few times a year would be in his own name.

"What's keeping you?" Maureen called up the stairs.

"Coming."

He opened the flask and drank two mouthfuls before leaving it unstoppered on the bedside table.

"How is he?" she asked when he came down.

"Fast asleep. I left the flask at his elbow in case he wakes up thirsty."

"I'll come back right away after the breakfast to see if he wants anything."

"Don't worry, he'll be all right on his own for a couple of hours," he said, getting into the car.

The wedding service went smoothly. Elizabeth was only five minutes late and, contrary to Kevin's expectations, O'Flaherty arrived on time. Kevin heard little of the service. His thoughts were on the ashen face on the pillow at home, and what prayers he said were not for Elizabeth and himself but for the old reprobate who had been a thorn in his flesh for so long.

After breakfast the drinking began in earnest. The men clung together with oily-looking whiskey glasses in their scarred hands, and the women surrounded Elizabeth and the bridesmaids like wasps about a jam jar. Later, when the men had consumed their share of drink, the more self-satisfied would turn uxorious and the more self-confident adulterous, but the women would be sufficiently womanly to encourage them both to act out their dreams in dancing. Meanwhile, those who enjoyed the rough edge of manly conversation would make a last stand against the efforts of the women to get them onto the dance floor, while a few rare fellows who thought that conversation was not everything would sing a song. Kevin stayed with the men, trying to attend to their jokes with one half of his mind and wondering with the other half when Maureen would go home and discover that their father was dead. O'Flaherty was at his most conversable, going from group to group, regaling them with his favourite stories about "his friend the A.I. man" and returning to Kevin every now and then with a word of comradely concern.

"As best man I consider it my final duty today to make sure that you are fit to perform tonight. The knack is to drink the right amount. Drink too little and you'll be too nervous. Drink too much and you won't be able to find it. It's a matter of fine tolerance, and I'm determined to make sure that you get it right. Here, have another drink!"

To escape the torrent of advice, Kevin went into the toilet only to find Billy Snoddy enjoying a solitary pee, waving his uncircumcised cock around as if he were watering a flowerbed with a hose pipe. Though he had been drinking for only an hour, he had had enough. Kevin felt uneasy in his company. He did not wish to antagonize him today, but neither did he wish to appear placatory.

"This is where all the big nobs hang out." Snoddy laughed at the hackneyed joke as if he had minted it on the spot.

"The interesting thing about nobs is that they all, or nearly all, piss equally well," Kevin said to appear light-hearted.

"You're saying that the difference between a good one and a bad one lies elsewhere?"

"It's a difference that is not apparent to the naked eye."

"Yet it's very real to women. And if you asked them

122

why, they would slap your face. I've often wondered what women really think of them."

"Maybe they don't think of them," Kevin ventured.

"There are women who think of them and women who don't. I would say myself that Elizabeth Hurley née Quane does not."

"I was pleased the rain held off," said Kevin.

"A happy marriage is one where the man and the woman are equally proud of the member that is their common property."

"I must tell Maureen to go home and make sure the oul' fellah is all right."

"Kevin Hurley, your member is no longer your own. A licensed bull is a tethered bull."

"Don't forget your jobs this evening, will you?"

"If you like, I'll drive Maureen home now. It might keep me from drinking more than is good for either of us."

Kevin weighed the possibilities and, as the least of several evils, put his hand in his pocket for the car keys.

Determined to have one more drink before news of death put a stopper on the nuptials, he joined Festus in the bar while Snoddy went off with Maureen. After a while Elizabeth came in and said that she wanted a word with him. She was in a turquoise going-away suit with a turquoise ribbon in her hair and rarely worn stiletto heels that brought the tip of her nose to the level of his shoulder. Noticing for the first time the brown flecks in the grey of her eyes, he could not believe that she was his wife; she was no more his wife today than yesterday or last week. He had married her only to find that she was still as elusive as a moor hen in a boghole, but he smiled at her, telling himself that he must have been naive to imagine that the familiar formula recited over them by McGladdery could confer on him a sense of possession and companionship which would only come, if at all, from years, maybe a life, of shared living. Or could it come from one hallucinatory night of shared sexuality?

"We should be making plans to leave," she said in the hallway.

"But the fun has only started. People are just beginning to get the flavour."

"The flavour of whiskey. You've been to weddings before. You know that they all end with too many men having too much to drink. We must leave before the merry din becomes a drunken rout. And remember, you've got to drive to Galway."

"That won't take long."

"Have you booked a hotel?"

"There's no need, it's not races week."

"If we haven't got a hotel, we'd better get there early."

"We don't need a hotel. I know a big Tipperary woman who runs a guesthouse in Salthill and puts me up whenever I go to the races. We'll go there."

"No, we won't, we'll go to a hotel. I want privacy on my wedding night. I know what Nosy Parkers landladies are. I've had enough of them in Dublin. What's the best hotel in Galway?"

"The Great Southern."

"We'll go there for our hibernation hymeneal."

"What's that?"

"A code word for honeymoon. We don't want every Harry, Dick and Tom to know our business."

"Well, certainly not Harry and Tom."

"It's settled then."

"The Great Southern is expensive, full of Americans willing to pay through the nose for lobster served under its French name but supposedly caught by an Irish-speaking Aran islander."

"All right, we'll have lobster tonight in the Great Southern. If it pleases you, you can have *gliomach ar an sean nós* while I have *homard à la Newburg*."

He could not help smiling at her spirited self-assertion, especially when he remembered that they would be spending the night at a wake surrounded by sympathetic neighbours, not tip-obsessed flunkeys.

"I want you to name a time for leaving now and I want you to stick to it. It's the only way I'll get you out of here in fit condition for the road."

"All right, we'll leave at four," he said in the knowledge that it did not matter.

Billy Snoddy came through the swing doors and straight towards them. "I've got bad news for you, Kevin. Your father's dead."

"When did he die?"

"He was cold when we got home, but he must have woken up after we left. The stopper wasn't in the flask and the tea inside had gone down."

"I'm sorry," Elizabeth said, taking his hand.

"We'll go home right away—as soon as I've told Festus and the rest," he said.

"It had to happen to us," she said when they were alone in the car.

"He had to die sometime. He just chose the wrong day."

"What will we do now?"

"We'll go home and shake hands with all who come to the wake."

"Like any long-married man and wife?"

"When the wake is over, we'll go to the funeral, and the day after the funeral we'll go to Galway for whatever it was you said."

"Won't people think it too soon?" she suggested.

125

"No, he was an old man. It isn't as if his death was unexpected."

Maureen washed the body and pared the toenails and fingernails, and when she had finished, Kevin shaved the hollow cheeks, pointed chin and stringy gills with his old bone-handled cutthroat. They tidied the room, put fresh linen on the bed, lit a blessed candle on each side of a crucifix, and twined a pair of black rosary beads round his big-jointed fingers.

"It was a lovely death in the heel of the hunt," Maureen said when they had finished. "He went quietly, like a swan going downriver. His legs were stretched straight, his eyes and mouth closed, and his hands joined in front of him. It was as if he didn't want to cause trouble, as if he decided to lay himself out without a helping hand from anyone."

"Billy Snoddy said that he had a swig of tea before leaving."

"He had an' all. What surprised me was that he didn't have more—after all the whiskey I put in it this morning."

No sooner had they finished than the first neighbours came in. Kevin and Elizabeth drove to Killage to order a coffin and buy drink and food for the visitors—sweet sherry for the women, whiskey, beer, and stout for the men, two large hams, seven pounds of tomatoes, eight loaves, four barm bracks, butter and jam.

On the way back Elizabeth asked, "Will you be staying up all night?"

"No. I'll go to bed after the rosary. I feel tired after the day."

"Where will you sleep?"

"I think we should both sleep at Larch Lawn. It will be quieter."

"It won't look callous?"

"Even in the shadow of death, life, such as it is, must go on," he replied.

After they had said the rosary at midnight, he and Elizabeth drove to Larch Lawn. She made him coffee and sandwiches, and he sat at the kitchen table looking at pictures of weddings in the local newspaper, while she opened and closed doors upstairs.

"I've put you in Murt's old room," she said when she came down again.

"And where will you sleep?"

"In my own room."

"On your own?"

"If you don't mind."

"It's a strange start to a marriage." He tried to laugh.

"I'm . . . not feeling well."

"Is it what my mother used to call the plague?"

"Yes."

"Well, it was you who named the day." He smiled.

"Normally, I'm reasonably regular, but this time, when it mattered, I was six days late."

He went across to the settee and put his arm round her shoulders. He did not love her, but he wanted to possess her, to make her his own and rid himself at once of the enfeebling feeling that he was her chauffeur. He wanted to feel that she was his wife, because he knew that he would not get a wink of innocent sleep until her warmly encompassing folds had bled him of his seed.

"It's nearly over," she continued. "We could go to bed together, I suppose, but you might be shocked."

"We'll sleep together if only to get used to each other."

"On second thoughts, I don't think so. I'd like my wedding night to be perfect. We'll wait till after the funeral, and then we'll go to bed properly, between starched sheets in the Great Southern."

He kissed her on the lips, but he could tell from the stiffness of them that she was eager to escape from him, so he said good night and trudged upstairs alone. Before he fell asleep, he found himself wondering how any man manages to invade a woman outside matrimony, because even with a licence the going seemed tough enough to daunt anyone except Festus O'Flaherty. Then he thought of Maureen, of her natural openness, her earthy intuition, her unerring way with a man, and he told himself, There are heifers and there are fillies, and you've married a filly.

On Tuesday morning, after his father had been kibbed for twenty-four hours, he and Elizabeth set off for Galway, first crossing the Delour River and driving over Slieve Bloom in the direction of Kinnitty. It was a lovely morning of soft breezes, with a regatta of white clouds sailing before them against a sea-blue sky, and the flat countryside, a jigsaw of different greens, falling away behind them as they climbed the mountain road. Around them rose a forest of deeper green with a hint of intersecting triangles as the conifers stood to attention one above the other like an army of immovable sentinels. Then the road began to dip, and they found themselves on the other side of Slieve Bloom with another landscape laid like a table before them.

"We'll have a drink in Birr to shorten the journey," he said when they had passed Kinnitty.

"But surely that will only lengthen it."

"We're on holiday. We can forget about the clock for a day or two. Apart from going to the races and the All-Ireland and once to a wedding in London, I've never been on holiday before."

He drank two pints of stout in Birr while she sipped a dry sherry and told him that she considered stout a cow's drink, that she failed to understand how anyone except a cow could drink a pint let alone two. He explained to her with more good humour than he felt justified that it all had to do with the circumference of the gullet, that while a thimbleful of sherry might wet a woman's, nothing less than half a gallon would lubricate a man's.

"But there are men who drink sherry!" she said triumphantly.

"And there are women who drink stout. Of the two, I prefer the women."

"Why is that?"

"Because I have more in common with them."

"I thought you were going to say that it is more natural to err on the side of coarseness than refinement."

"No, let it be remembered that it was you who said that," he replied, sucking the froth from the bottom of his glass.

As they crossed the spreading Shannon, he said, "Now, we're really on holiday, we're in Connacht."

"It's after two. We'd better eat in Portumna," she replied.

They went into the first hotel they saw, a brooding building with dark corridors and an empty dining room with a picture of President Kennedy on one wall and Pope John XXIII on another. They sat at a table by the only window and counted the bonhams in the lorry that was parked outside. Three policemen with beefy necks came in and sat at the table nearest the kitchen. A red-haired waitress came backwards through the swing doors and placed a plate of soup before each policeman while the youngest and beefiest of them patted her flat bottom.

"Lunch is finished," she told Kevin as she picked up the menu from his table.

"What about the policemen?" he asked.

"They're regulars. They eat here every day."

"We've been travelling and we're absolutely famished. Have you anything at all that we could eat?" Elizabeth inquired.

"I'll ask cook," she said, and off she went.

"If you'd done without your stout in Birr, we'd have been in time for lunch," she observed. He did not reply, because, though a husband of only four days' standing, he already knew that enigmatic abstraction is the best answer to fifty per cent of a wife's observations.

"You can have tomato soup, roast mutton, carrots and mashed potatoes, with stewed pears to follow," the waitress said when she returned.

"It will do," said Elizabeth.

The tomato soup, carrots, and pears came out of a tin; the mutton was fatty, tough and cold; and the potatoes, which were the colour of old parsnips, contained hard little nodules which, according to Elizabeth, must have been added deliberately by the cook after mashing. No sooner had the policemen finished their meal than the waitress came out of the kitchen with a vacuum cleaner and began cleaning the carpet around their table.

"This is too much," said Elizabeth. "First they try to poison us with braxy and then they deafen us. Don't they realize that we're on honeymoon?"

"Perhaps they do."

"Would you please stop Hoovering till we've eaten," she said to the waitress.

"Sorry, ma'am, I can't. Cook said that I must get the room ready for tonight. The Macra are having their annual dinner."

"And I hope they have their annual lecture on foggage to go with it," she said, turning to Kevin.

The lunch had been an eye-opener for him. Though he

disapproved of the lack of beef and mustard and thought the potatoes abominable, he was willing to eat and be thankful. He was not going to allow Irish hotel cuisine to impair his exhilarating sense of freedom, which, he felt, must surely come from the awareness that he had just been spancelled. Elizabeth, on the other hand, had lost her sense of proportion. She was evincing all the signs of middle-class horror, as if she might summon the hotel manager at any moment. Was this because she was a woman? Or was it because she lacked his philosophic calm, which would never be ruffled by braxy mutton or the hard nodules that Irish chefs secrete in mashed potatoes? It was a vision of her he would remember. As Festus said, in the battle of the sexes every potsherd of experience, every tittle of intelligence about the enemy must be turned to immediate and devastating account.

They arrived in Galway to find the streets glistening after rain. The Great Southern was comfortable and thickly carpeted, and their commodious bedroom looked down on the open square. After tea and biscuit, Elizabeth had a bath and, when she had finished, she suggested that Kevin should follow suit. It seemed a reasonable thought, and as he lay in the warm water making waves with his hand so that his penis floated to and fro like an exotic sea plant in a tangle of seaweed, he considered the end and purpose of the day, the night of sexuality to come. Even now, a mere five hours away, it seemed impossible. But after the first hesitant tacking, the wind would stand fair forevermore. Who knew, perhaps tomorrow she would be forward enough to invite him for a romp in the bath.

After a good dinner at the hotel, a walk down Shop Street, and a drink in the lounge, they went to bed. He got in between the sheets before her and waited in fresh pyjamas with his face to the window, wondering if virgins were as tricky as some old farmers made out. At last she switched off the light and crawled in beside him like a stray dog looking for shelter. He put his arms round her and stroked her hair and breasts, then kissed her on the lips and drew her towards him till her groin met his own. She was a mature, sophisticated woman, he told himself, a woman who had turned her back on her own kind and had come to him, a spreading oak that would shelter her in weaving branches. If it was an oak she wanted, he would not be a weeping willow. He would be strong. He would deny himself, give her plenty of time, perhaps an hour and a half, to overcome her virgin modesty. He would keep Fagin under covers, hold him in leash until the last minute; and then, when she had felt the naked heat of him, she would open wide the city gates, desiring nothing more than his lion-spring within her.

He reached down and pulled up her silk nightdress, then caressed her belly and little bum with his left hand. It was her bum that undid him. The two cheeks were so small that he could span them with the fingers of one hand, and the feeling it gave him of being lord of a whole galaxy made Fagin so impatient that he could not be denied. With the flick of a magician drawing a rabbit from a hat, he brought him out of his pyjamas and laid him uncompromisingly between her thighs. The stiffening of her body and the heaving of her shoulders began at the same time. He kissed her quickly to find tears running down her cheeks.

"What's wrong, Elizabeth?" he whispered.

"I'm not a virgin," she said between sobs.

"Why must you be so honest?" he asked in despair.

"I wanted you to know the truth."

"That you're foggage?"

"Foggage?"

"You know! Grass after the first cutting. Autumn foggage isn't as rich in nutrients as spring grass, but I'm not complaining. You'll have to do."

132

"You don't understand," she said. "It was not my fault. I was raped by an English journalist called Alexander Utley, and when it was all over he told me that it was only symbolic, that he was re-enacting the Tudor conquest of Ireland. Do you believe me, Kevin?"

"I do," he said for the second time in a week, "but there are those who wouldn't."

"I want to sleep now," she said.

"Sleep away," he replied and turned his back on her.

He woke in the night to find her bottom in his crotch, his arms round her waist, and his face buried in her perfumed hair. He held a breast in each hand, weighing them like pokes of gold dust, and she turned and kissed his closed eyes.

"You'll have to be gentle with me," she whispered. "I've had one bad experience and I don't want another, but if we lie together and fondle each other, I'll get used to you bit by bit. It's just that when I feel it between my legs, I shiver."

"I'll wait till you're ready," he said, and immediately wondered if he meant it.

Their honeymoon was like no honeymoon he had ever heard of. They spent the days motoring about Connemara, stopping off to sit on wind-scoured beaches, cross rocky stretches of mean land, or to drink a sour pint in a wayside pub. It was an alien country with an alien people, and after one day he longed for rich acres and powdery clay and the company of men who made a good living from good land. Elizabeth, on the other hand, seemed to find spiritual rest in the harshness of the life. She wore a headscarf like the women, watched wildlife for hours on end, and spoke endearingly to wild-eyed schoolchildren. They came back to the hotel in the evenings for a late dinner, and after a drink in the bar they would go to bed. Elizabeth always read for an hour before turning off the light, and he waited in the knowledge that she was her own woman, that nothing he could now do would change her.

In the centrally heated darkness he would fondle her for an hour and maybe rest the long-suffering Fagin between her thighs. One night he was so exhausted that he himself fell asleep while Fagin kept vigil in her silk knickers, and when he woke again she was kissing his cheek and madly biting his earlobe, and Fagin was safely ensconced inside her.

"I put him in myself while you slept," she said. "But don't move yet. Just leave him as he is, resting warmly and snugly for a second."

After a time they both began to move together like driftwood on a turning tide. As he thrust against softness, there was vengeance and harshness in his heart, and then he saw the warm water of the Gulf Stream lifting a rare sea plant in a fringe of seaweed, and he discharged.

What a relief! At long last, for better or worse, they were man and wife, and the headlines in *The Leinster Express* would not shout, MARRIAGE ANNULLED. FOGGAGE LECTURER FAILS TO CONSUMMATE. It was the most wonderful thing that had ever happened to him. It was like passing your driving test after failing ten times, after giving up all hope of success.

"We can go home now," he said.

"It was worth waiting," she replied.

Part Two

8

Throughout her twenties, living in lonely bed-sitters in Dublin, Elizabeth longed for a man who would sweep her off her feet. She knew that marriage was something that would never come easy to her, but she felt that the right man would be powerful enough to shield her from what she imagined to be the horrors of it. She waited and waited, but the man with powers to sweep never appeared. Instead, she had gone out with a succession of weedy little men—solicitors' clerks, naive young doctors, chartered accountants, and civil engineers—men who loved themselves with single-minded determination and sought a woman to help them love themselves even more. She had become accustomed to little men from life's infantry, so she was anything but prepared for an English technical journalist called Alexander Utley.

He arrived unexpectedly with the force of Strongbow and the self-confidence of a lieutenant-colonel, and before she could pronounce his unlikely name her hymen was a broken cobweb, a flimsy piece of gossamer on a wilting stick. For that she did not blame Utley but her unworldly upbringing at Larch Lawn, followed by a cold convent, silly girl friends, and empty afternoons in the desert she found in Dublin. In her innocence she had dreamt of upright men of unimpeachable ideals, men who would seek her out for the clarity of her intellect and the purity of her character, men who would not only talk but listen and in the simplicity of her conversation hear the echo of a chord which they had hitherto sought in vain. Utley flattered her into thinking that he had heard the chord and wished to hear it again. In the summer dusk he spoke from beneath a mantle of English idealism, bemused her with talk of the essential fidelity of Albion, and left her smarting with an uncharacteristic suspicion of men. For months she lived entirely among women, until the resultant ennui drove her to a dance in the Four Courts.

"Are you a solicitor by any chance?" asked a barrister who had trodden twice on her toes.

"No, I'm a schoolteacher."

"What a pity." He smiled. Then he quickly looked at his watch and said, "I'm only here for a brief or two."

She was so taken by his unprofessional line in self-ridicule that she forgave him his clumsiness and took him home to meet Attracta Craig, with whom she shared a flat in a red-brick house in Ballsbridge. Attracta never went to dances. She sat at home reading Byron as a funnel-web spider might sit at home weaving, and whenever Elizabeth invited a young man back for coffee, Attracta would close the collected letters of His Lordship and ask the unfortunate fellow if he played the hurdy-gurdy. As she waited for his hesitant reply, she would roll her bulbous eyes and uncross her legs so that her nylons rustled against her underskirt and the fragrance of freesia filled the room. The fragrance invariably unnerved the young men, none of whom knew the precise meaning of hurdy-gurdy and not a few of whom obviously thought that it had something to do with unnatural sex. Then Attracta would ask the visitor if he had heard of Anthony Van Hoboken, and when he said no, she would explain at great length that Hoboken was a Dutch musicologist who compiled a catalogue of Haydn's music and, more important, that Haydn composed for the hurdy-gurdy.

Soon the young man would be appealing to Elizabeth for rescue or wondering when it would be politic to leave. Elizabeth would do her best with coffee and biscuits to re-cover their pre-Hoboken sense of togetherness, but Attracta would administer the coup de grace with a question about what Pitt the Younger and Guillaume Lekeu had in common. After an uncomfortable silence, she would tell the young man that something important happened to them both at twenty-four, that Pitt the Younger became prime minister and Lekeu died of typhoid. Following a *tour d'horizon* of Lekeu's musical career, the young man would try to laugh, but neither biscuits nor coffee, neither chocolate-backed digestives nor freshly ground mocha, could medicine him into self-forgetfulness; and he would invariably hurry away after a half-hearted kiss in the hallway, stumbling down the garden path as if pursued by Medusa.

On the way back to Ballsbridge, Elizabeth was careful to brief her barrister before introducing him to Attracta. She told him that Attracta was a dear friend who must be humoured in her tiresome obsession with the hurdy-gurdy, Hoboken and Lekeu. The barrister said nothing, but when Attracta asked him about the hurdy-gurdy, he told her that he once heard it played beautifully in Spain by a butch les-bian. Then all became clear to Elizabeth. Her young men had evidently thought that both she and Attracta were queer, and it occurred to her that that was what Attracta had meant them to think.

She was so grateful to her barrister that she went out with him six times in a fortnight and invited him to Larch Lawn for Whit weekend. He seemed to get on like a house on fire with Murt, but after he left on Sunday evening Murt told her not to invite him again.

"Why?" she asked in amazement.

"Because he made a pass at me in the bathroom this morning."

It was the last straw. She stopped going to dances, and soon she stopped going out with men altogether. After a year she could bear Dublin no longer, so she said goodbye to Attracta and came back to teach in Killage, resigned to the limitations of country life and the indignities of spinsterhood in a society of men-befriending men and pregnant women. She immersed herself in teaching during the day and music in the evenings, while always in the background, coming and going, busy with his own life, was her brother Murt. Without him she could not have survived. She cooked his evening meal and washed his shirts and asked him every day what he had been doing on the farm; and he did his jobs in the yard and in the fields, ate his food without comment, and now and again told her a piece of gossip. She was always grateful when he told her something, even something in which she was not interested, because it showed that he considered her his equal, that he did not think that only men could make men's talk. Their conversations never took wing, however. They consisted of a single statement followed by a single comment, or a statement followed by questions and laconic answers.

"Donie Dunne died last night," he might say as she poured his tea.

"What did he die of?" she would ask.

"Constipation."

And if she replied that the whole country was dying of

constipation, he would merely say, "I only know what Young Dunne told me."

With him there was never any possibility of going from the particular to the general, of pushing a conversation out of its familiar shape for the sheer delight of creating surprise or laughter. He did not make conversation; he made statements which, if they were to be made at all, had to be seen by him to be self-evident. Yet he did not lack intelligence or imagination; he merely aspired to the condition of silence. He saw each remark as a balloon which must not be allowed to rise, but must be pricked and replaced by an entirely new balloon, which in turn must be replaced as soon as possible by another. To talk to him, therefore, was to officiate at the birth and violent death of at least five conversations in as many minutes. It was as if the lines of his thought converged unfailingly on a point rather than widened into multifariousness, as if he never had an association of ideas, never saw an unlikely yet revealing relationship. She might have found this irritating, but she didn't. She accepted his ways, even to the extent of enjoying his "conversation." Talking to him had become a game for her, the object of which was to deny him the opportunity of puncturing the balloon. It was a game at which she was near adept, at least sufficiently adept to keep the balloon aloft for all of fifty seconds.

When she first came home, she would sometimes go to a neighbour's house to ramble, but there she found herself among women who talked of nothing but child-bearing, child-rearing, disease, and sudden death. At mealtimes the men would come in with talk of cattle and crops, filling the stuffy kitchen with the fragrance of open fields, with meadowsweet, hawthorn, and new-mown hay. But they were jealous of their fragrance. They kept it to themselves, never sharing it with what in their eyes was all too plainly the "weaker sex." She would have liked to talk seriously to the men about the cattle mart, about how to judge the beefing quality of a bullock by its conformation, but because they were as likely to talk to her about dry stock as Wittgenstein she gave up her forays into neighbours' houses and confined herself to things she could do alone. Once or twice she tried to have a farming conversation with Kevin and Murt, and when they laughed incredulously she took to making jokes about timothy, cocksfoot, and fescue, which they found more acceptable, because it endowed her in their eyes with a recognizable "personality."

Her half-conscious life might have lasted into old age if Murt had lived. His death brought her the pain of self-awareness and the realization that she'd loved him as she had loved no other man, that his words were more precious for being so few, that she was now without a cloak on a cold day. When the wake and the funeral were over and the house was quiet again, she looked round and saw not people but cattle. On her walk to the Grove after school, for every man she met she counted threescore bullocks. Clearly, if she wished to live here, she would have to live like the men, through the medium of cattle.

In an odd way the discovery pleased her. She would become a farmer, and as a farmer she would be taken seriously. Her land and house, her crops and herd would furnish her with a recognizable personality in public places. She would attend farmers' meetings, ploughing matches, land auctions, and agricultural shows, and if she wished to talk to her foreman about the beefing quality of a bullock, he would nod respectfully and feel the loose fat between the animal's hind legs, behind the spot where the scrotum used to hang. She would not draw attention to herself by becoming a farmer overnight, however. She would continue to teach for a time, until she had acquired enough knowledge to wear a pair of dirty Wellingtons with the natural confidence of a man.

The first few months were a time of pain. She missed Murt as she might miss an amputated leg or arm, but gradually the business of supervising the running of the farm took her mind off the emptiness in her heart. Then Kevin was an invaluable support. He reminded her of Murt. He had Murt's laconic turn of phrase, his seriousness about land and cattle, and his bland unawareness of everything else in the world. At first she saw him as a man who drew strength from his limitations, from his ability to conserve his conversational ingenuity, to make one word go a long way. She felt that it would take a lifetime to get to know him, for the simple reason that he doled himself out in drops, not coffee spoons. He would sit at her kitchen table, silent between sentences and unaware of his silence, while she wondered what on earth to say to him. Admittedly, she had invited him to discuss farming, but even farming conversation sometimes flags, and soon she had to speak to him through music, which, she knew, must surely illumine the purity of his innocent soul. After a month she began to sense that he came to her to lay some dark personal burden on her shoulders, and though he never said a word about himself she knew that she had lit a spark in his life as indeed he had lit one in hers.

His effect on her was purely physical, having as much to do with his distinctive personal smell as his personality. He never had a bath, she knew; yet he never smelt of sweat. He was one of those men, mentioned ironically by Montaigne, who are naturally sweet-smelling, or, more accurately, who smell of the rain-washed earth. Whenever he left the room, he left a hint of himself behind, which tantalized her into wishing that she could throw away her eau de cologne and rosewater and take on with him the smell of tilled fields and trodden grass. Then she would tell herself that she must not romanticize the man, that he was a farmer in dirty Wellingtons, more at home talking to heifers than women, insensitive to all ways of life except his own. She told herself that life with him would pummel and bruise her, but when he asked her to marry him she never for one moment thought of saying no.

When she moved into Clonglass, what surprised her most was the character of the house. She could not believe that one house could differ so much from another only a quarter of a mile away. It was an old two-storey stone-built house with small deep-set windows that revealed the uncommon thickness of the walls. The kitchen was the most distinctive room, large and dark, with a flagged floor, an old but comfortable chaise longue bought long ago at some country auction, and a big black range with lion's feet on which stood a variety of blackened pots and pans and above which hung a clothesline laden with socks, shirts, and towels. In one corner was a lovely pinewood dresser with large plates bearing pictures of rivers and anglers and cattle drinking, and in another was a television set which no one watched except Maureen, while on the shelf by the window was a small wireless which was turned on twice a day, once for the weather forecast in the morning and again for the weather forecast at bedtime. The life of the household found its keenest expression in the kitchen. Here meals were cooked and eaten, and here Kevin lay on the chaise longue by the range at the end of the day while Maureen knitted and watched television and Snoddy swallowed and read the local newspaper.

Behind the kitchen was the parlour, a large damp uninhabited room with a round mahogany table and six high-backed chairs in the centre and a sewing machine in one corner. By the window was a leather-covered sofa and by the opposite wall was a small sideboard where Maureen kept her best china and Kevin kept his ale and whiskey. On the low mantelpiece were an assortment of family photographs and two shields and a cup that Kevin had won for clay-pigeon shooting. No one used the parlour except at Christmas, wakes, and weddings. It was a private shrine dedicated to an obscure family history and without which the house would no longer be itself. Breathing its musty, immobile air on her first day, Elizabeth opened the window and let in the enlivening breath of summer.

She had come to alien territory. While Larch Lawn was open, sunny, and smiling, commanding a view of the road to Killage, Clonglass hunkered behind trees and hedges that enclosed the inhabitants in a sheltered maze. However, the look of the house gave only the merest intimation of the brooding life within. Kevin went about his work in silence while Maureen chattered and Billy Snoddy watched everyone else with the alert cunning of a dog fox. On the first day she merely observed and said nothing, but by evening she had realized that she could do one of two things: fall in with their badgerlike ways and become one of them or by imposing her own ideas on them bring light and sanity to the house. In her favour was the fact that the enemy was plain to be seen—it was Maureen. It was with Maureen that she would have to struggle for supremacy in the kitchen, a struggle in which she would get little solace from Kevin, who saw the house merely as a place to eat and sleep in. The open world of the fields was his kingdom and all else was at best a source of distraction. So it would have to be a struggle between women, and she sensed that in this house a woman's business was soon done.

Mealtimes provided the first bone of contention. Kevin seemed to eat nothing but beef, beef made uneatable by an excess of English mustard. For their first meal together she cooked lamb stew, and when she gave him the first plateful Maureen laughed and said, "God mend your wit, you poor misguided woman. Sure, that man has tasted no meat but beef for the last three years."

"He tasted braxy mutton in Portumna," said Elizabeth, feeling foolish at having shown such ignorance of her husband, and at the same time certain that for her sake Kevin would eat the stew. But all he said was "Where's that beef, Maureen?" and cut himself six thick slices from the joint.

To add to her troubles she was still teaching and therefore absent from the midday meal five days a week, which meant that from Monday to Friday Maureen cooked the main meal of the day, that in a sense she was still the housekeeper. Elizabeth asked Kevin to have something light at lunchtime, bread and cheese perhaps, and to postpone dinner so that she herself could cook it in the evening, but he told her succinctly that only men who didn't have to work for a living have dinner in the evening.

"Could *you* plough a whole afternoon on a ploughman's lunch?" he asked. "The only people who eat ploughman's lunch are city slickers who wouldn't know the difference between a frog and a coulter."

As she was at home all day on Saturday and Sunday, she wished to make the weekend dinners as memorable as she could. On the first Sunday she cooked them her favourite dish, goulash with paprika and yoghurt, and she was pleased to see that Kevin ate with relish. She was aware that Maureen was a rough-and-ready cook, that she served boiled potatoes in their jackets, parsnips in cubes and swedes in thick slices. As a little refinement which might show up Maureen, she mashed the parsnips with nutmeg and cream and the swedes with black pepper and butter, and in an ill-disguised attempt to elicit compliments she asked Kevin if he could taste the nutmeg in the parsnips.

"They taste more of parsnips than anything else," he said, and Maureen and Billy Snoddy laughed at her discomfiture.

It was a cloudy afternoon and the four of them sat round

the table in semidarkness because Kevin had just reminded them of the high cost of electricity. As he believed not only in dry but silent "packing," Maureen and Snoddy were left to make most of the conversation, and most of their conversation was low. During the week she had mentioned it to Kevin, but he merely said that he had heard no low conversation, that Maureen and Snoddy spoke far too loudly for his taste. One of the allusions that came up oftenest and puzzled her most was the "Lad in the Corner." Whenever Maureen referred to him, Snoddy would break into a paroxysm of belly laughter and Kevin would look serious and concentrate with greater force on his plate.

Halfway through the Sunday dinner Maureen and Snoddy began telling dirty jokes. Maureen started it by asking Snoddy if he had heard the one about the housewife from Kinnitty who gave a coathanger to the A.I. man for his trousers, and Snoddy responded with a story about a man from Borris who could tell the time by looking between a horse's hind legs.

Maureen and Snoddy spluttered with laughter, and Kevin laid down his fork and knife and laughed too. Elizabeth was horrified to find Kevin revelling in such bawdy, and she said that if she heard another dirty story she would eat alone in the parlour.

"Then, I'll tell a clean story," said Billy Snoddy, "clean because there's no sex in it." And he began a long scatological story about a tobacconist from Camross who made excellent snuff by putting dried horse dung through his wife's coffee grinder.

"Enough is enough," said Elizabeth, getting up from the table.

"Hold your horses, woman," said Kevin.

"What are you going to say to them?" she demanded.

"There will be no more dirty stories at table. Anyone

who feels that he must release one will go out and do it in the yard."

Maureen and Snoddy laughed at what they took to be a double entendre, and Elizabeth sat down again in the knowledge that without Kevin she was helpless.

Gradually, however, she managed to introduce several little changes as a civilizing influence in the house. In his passion for thrift, Kevin had decreed that the toilet paper at Clonglass should be two-column strips of *The Leinster Express,* and it was only after much argument about personal hygiene and the sensitivity of the female fundament that he agreed to her buying soft two-ply tissue from the supermarket. She bought an electric cooker with her own money, because she found that she could not master the timing of meals on the range, and she began lighting fires in the parlour to dry the damp walls and the musty air so that she could make the room her own while waiting for Kevin to build her music room.

The lack of anything that could be called music at Clonglass was one of the things that offended her most. Sometimes in the morning Maureen would listen to Irish dance music on the radio while waiting for the weather forecast, and whenever this happened Elizabeth would have her breakfast in the parlour, because there was nothing she abhorred more than the never-ending diddle-diddle-diddle of Irish music on Radio Eireann. The fiddle and the accordion were like the mist on Slieve Bloom, monotonous and eternal, filling the pit of her stomach with a dull cheerless ache. She had asked Kevin to bring her piano from Larch Lawn, but he said that he was too busy just then, that he would see to it the following week. She began going to Larch Lawn to play in the evenings, but as that was too much of a nuisance, she got Billy Snoddy and John Noonan to move the piano while Kevin was at the mart. After much huffing and puffing they put it on the trailer, but when they reached Clonglass, they found that it would not go through the parlour door.

"We'll have to take out the doorjamb," she said.

"We can't do that till Kevin comes home," said Maureen.

"You're right," said Snoddy. "It's a decision for the man of the house and no one else."

Helpless, she watched them carry out the piano again and stand it in the shed between a cultivator and a mower. She felt raw with defeat, with the awareness of having been mistress of her own house and farm while now she was less than a wife, and to soothe her nerves she sat between the cultivator and the mower, playing from memory Brahms's intermezzo in E flat major.

"It's a wonder you wouldn't play something we can all hum, 'Galway Bay' or 'The Mountains of Mourne,'" Kevin said when he returned from the mart. It was the sort of thing he would not have said a month ago. While courting her, he sat in silence through Bach, Beethoven, and Brahms as if they had transported him beyond the vulgarity of mere comment.

"I want you to put the piano in the parlour. We tried but it wouldn't go in the door. We may have to tear out the jamb, I'm afraid."

"Have you tried getting it through the right way?" he asked.

"I didn't try. I left it to Billy Snoddy and John Noonan."

"I don't know about Noonan, but Snoddy has two left feet."

After trial and error and an irreverent commentary from Maureen, Kevin and Snoddy managed to get the piano through the door, only to find that there was no room for it inside.

"We'll have to move the sewing machine," said Elizabeth.

"It's my sewing machine and it was Mammy's before me," said Maureen.

"How often do you use it?" Kevin asked.

"Maybe a dozen times a year."

"How often do you play the piano?" he asked Elizabeth.

"Every day."

"Then, we'll put the piano in the parlour and the sewing machine in the shed, at least till I get time to build a music room."

"A judgement of Solomon," said Billy Snoddy, opening his frog's mouth in silent laughter.

It was a victory for Elizabeth but a minor victory. She realized that without Kevin's backing she would have been defeated, because Snoddy would have acted on Maureen's instructions before he acted on hers.

"She's determined to humiliate me," she said to Kevin in bed that night. "I'm helpless, utterly helpless, in the face of her l.p.c."

"What's that for Christ's sake?"

"Low peasant cunning. She does everything she can to make me realize that this is her home, not mine. When I change things in the kitchen, she keeps changing them back, and she's dirty, she doesn't wash except on Sunday. I've been thinking. We'll never have a moment's peace together while she's here. She'd be better off helping Concepta in Roscrea or in service in Killage."

"I can't ask my sister to go into service. Maybe the answer is marriage."

"Marriage to whom?"

"I don't know."

"We must face the truth, Kevin. No sane man would marry her, she's so coarse. She and Snoddy are always laughing and spluttering over their food, and when you ask her what's so funny she says it's the Lad in the Corner. Who is the Lad in the Corner?''

"I don't know," he lied.

"I was certain you must. I thought it was a private joke between the three of you. You see, Kevin, I've begun to imagine things. That's what this house is doing to me."

In spite of the strain of the kitchen, she glowed in the privacy of the bedroom, stretched beside him in the dark listening to the sombre timbre of his voice. Compared with the chill and spiky years of spinsterhood, marriage was an intimation of something warm and soft, at least for a good part of the time. If only they had the house to themselves, she would open like a flower in the morning sun, cast off all girlish inhibitions, and see the earth perhaps as Kevin in his simple goodness saw it, with a bullock's eye or a horse's eye, bright and clean, unsullied by history, unfalsified by philosophy.

She hadn't rushed into marriage with both eyes closed; on the contrary she had approached it critically and with several reservations about the nature of sexual intimacy. She had feared that after years of self-denial she might be frigid, but experience soon proved that her worst fears were unjustified. Though Kevin enjoyed four orgasms to her one, she contented herself with the thought that it was early days and with thanking God that she had got over the first nervousness. And as she listened to his measured breathing in the dark, she would think that he would never know the nature of the things that he had unwittingly taught her. Sometimes she would wake up in the night to find him caressing her body with his hands as he slept. She would creep closer to him, basking in his warmth, reminding herself that she had finally put behind her the feelings of self-loathing that she had found to be the curse of spinsterhood.

151

When, after the first month, she discovered that she was pregnant, she was overjoyed. For some reason she expected that infertility should go with a tendency to frigidity, but now she had proved herself to be a woman in the fullest sense and she could not but warm to the man that had made her achievement possible.

She woke in the morning to find that he had left the bed. His place was cold; he was probably already giving the calves their mash. As she dressed, she noticed a blotch of grey skin between her toes, and when she examined the soles of her feet she found another ugly patch. She sat on the edge of the bed wondering what it could be. Was it to do with her pregnancy? Or was it to do with Clonglass? A germ from Maureen? A microbe picked up from Snoddy? She opened the bedroom window and took a deep breath with arms outstretched. The cool unhurrying air filled her lungs, and her head swam upwards, reminding her of a party in Dublin when a quantity surveyor whom she had admired briefly for his beard gave her her first cigarette.

9

Kevin had hoped that his marriage would clear the domestic air, but it only added a touch of sulphur. For the first few days after their honeymoon he managed to avoid being alone with Maureen, but when she goosed him playfully in the parlour, he knew that marriage meant nothing to her, that not even Elizabeth's presence in the house would stop her. Before he was back a week, she followed him into Rowan's Field and told him that being a "widow" did not agree with her, that a woman who is used to a regular poke needs to be weaned gradually. She wasn't sleeping at night, she was off her food, her bowels were bound and loose by turns, and she woke up with a blinding headache in the morning.

"But that's because you're pregnant!" He smiled.

"How many times have I to tell you that it was a false alarm? I've stopped having periods, which means that I'm always ready for you."

"Look, Maureen, I'm married now. It would be adultery as well as incest if I lay with you."

"Marriage has solved your problem but not mine. I'm at my wits' end. If you refuse to help, I'll have to turn to Snoddy, and you wouldn't like that now, would you?"

"I thought you had turned to him already."

"Dead mutton is no substitute for beef gristle."

He could not bear the thought of Snoddy spending his coppers at the first standing, so he promised to give her an average of two twankydillos a week for the first month, followed by one twankydillo a week for another two months. Then he would reduce the dosage to one a fortnight, and finally to one a month. When he told her that after six months she would have to do without, she said that his solution was more Catholic than Christian, that she would get better treatment from an Anglo-Irish Protestant.

Giving her what she considered to be her due wasn't easy. She could not come to his room at night because of Elizabeth, and he could not go to hers for the same reason. Elizabeth was at school during the day, but they could not go to bed after dinner because of Snoddy. As a makeshift solution, they devised a signal to fox him. Whenever Maureen was desperate, she would put a dollop of mustard on the side of his plate, while on other days she would leave it in the pot. On Mustard Days, as she called them, he would go out to the field with Snoddy after they had eaten and return later alone to give Maureen her glissando before the pianist came back from school at four.

To complicate matters, he was worried about the effect of ignoring the Foggage Principle. Now he had two women to satisfy and only a limited amount of oil in the tank. Unfortunately, he could not increase his sexual vigour by a liberal application of nitrogen, so the alternative was to introduce rationing. He had long been of the opinion that three times a week was enough for any God-fearing Christian. It was certainly enough for him, because he had found that if he did it more often he suffered agony in his back and briefcase. The answer was to limit Elizabeth to one a week, much though he disliked denying a newly married woman her sexual dues. Then, as he reduced Maureen's quota to one a week, he could give Elizabeth an extra tossication and show her that marriage improved with practice, that quite possibly the best was yet to be.

He now felt doubly guilty. He suffered not only from a sense of impending retribution for his incest with Maureen but also from an aching awareness of his betrayal of Elizabeth. His anxiety was aggravated by the constant bickering between the two of them. They even disagreed over which of them should darn his socks. Consequently, when he wanted something done, he often did it himself rather than give them further cause for wrangling.

Until he married Elizabeth he had not been aware of the special quality of his relationship with his sister. They were twins, they had grown up together in the same house, sharing every experience from swimming as children in the Grove river to grieving as adults over the death of their mother. They shared so many potent memories and knew each other's quirks so well that conversation formed only a small part of their communication. In fact, they knew each other so well that if they had been struck deaf and dumb for a month they would not have felt out of touch. In many ways Maureen was a more complex person than Elizabeth. She was a contradictory mixture of lust, religion, and superstition. Going to bed at night, she would pray to the Holy Souls to wake her at a certain time in the morning, and if he went to her bed and they came together, she would exclaim, "Jesus, Mary, and Joseph, it was like going up with Krakatoa." In her everyday round the saints were never far from her thoughts. If a hen was laying out, she would pray to St. Anthony to lead her to the nest, and if Monsignor was boring her with a lecture on systolic and diastolic pressure, she would say, "Sacred Heart of Jesus, for mercy's sake take him away." Though Kevin said none of these things, he had an instinctive understanding of them. He understood Maureen better than he understood Elizabeth.

He had no childhood memories of Elizabeth. Sex with her lacked old association. In bed with Maureen he would imagine her as a girl climbing a tree in the Grove with pink winceyette knickers down to her knees. But in bed with Elizabeth he had to live in the thinness of the present. She had spent her adolescence in a convent, and he knew nothing of her until she returned from Dublin five years ago. Their bodies were also different. While Maureen's was big and comfortable, generous as the earth and so round and full that your hand never felt a bone, Elizabeth's was thin and hard, appealing to the form-seeking intellect rather than the blood. Consequently, his blood told him at night that sex with his sister was more "natural" than sex with his wife, but in the morning the intellect would say that the blood led to darkness and death, that only conscience could point the way to light and life.

In the fields during the day he would puzzle over the contradictions of living and reiterate to himself that his first duty was to Elizabeth, who was carrying his child, possibly his son. He did his best to make her feel at home in Clonglass, but to his annoyance she remained ill at ease. Again and again she urged him to get rid of Maureen and Snoddy or, failing that, to move with her to Larch Lawn, where they would have a large modern house to themselves. He listened sympathetically and, without committing himself, told her that she must be patient, that Snoddy would go once the harvest was saved. Now that he had two farms to look after, he needed a farmhand more than ever, and good men were hard to get. She promised to be patient, but patience was not one of her virtues, a fact she clearly demonstrated during Judy's sickness.

She was fond of Judy, a big black Labrador that went with her everywhere. In the mornings the dog would accompany her to school, where she would lie in the hallway all day waiting for classes to end. Whenever Elizabeth drove to Killage to shop, Judy would sit beside her with her snout resting on the open window, sniffing the hedges and the rushing air. Kevin could understand her affection for the dog, especially when he remembered that Judy was the only company she had at Larch Lawn after Murt's death, but he was not prepared for her emotional behaviour when Judy became ill shortly after her move to Clonglass. Within a week of arrival, the dog began acting strangely. She lost her appetite, her stomach swelled, and her breath came to smell of rotten cabbage stumps. Elizabeth took her to Festus O'Flaherty, who promptly diagnosed severe constipation, due, he said, to the stress of moving from one house and townland to another. He dosed her with liquid paraffin and gave her an enema of soapy water to ease what he described as the "obstruction."

"I told you it was the move that caused it," Elizabeth said to Kevin when she came home. "I know because I haven't been too well myself."

"Nonsense, it was something she ate," he replied.

"Your friend O'Flaherty agrees with me."

"Even vets make mistakes." He left her fondling the dog.

Their problems had only begun, however. Judy began scratching her cheeks till they bled, then her sides till they were raw and weeping. This time Festus said that the dog was allergic to something at Clonglass and gave her an antihistamine injection. He continued to give her injections for three weeks but without any sign of improvement.

"It's a chronic allergy," he told Elizabeth. "And the problem, as you've found out, is that it's nigh impossible to discover the cause."

Elizabeth's reply was to take the dog to another vet, because, as she put it, "a male chauvinist is not the best vet to treat a bitch dog." The other vet confirmed O'Flaherty's diagnosis and recommended that she take the dog back to Larch Lawn to see if it would make any difference. This treatment recommended itself to Elizabeth, but at Larch Lawn the dog went from bad to worse. By August the poor animal was practically unrecognizable. She had begun chewing the pads of her feet till she could no longer walk without growling, and her sides were covered in running sores. One morning, while Elizabeth was at school, Kevin went to Larch Lawn to see the foreman and was so horrified by the dog's appearance that he resolved to take her to Festus right away.

"There's no cure for this," said O'Flaherty.

"Is there nothing else we can try?"

"How would you like to live like this?"

"I wouldn't wish it on my worst enemy," Kevin said.

"There's only one thing left to do—put her out of pain."

"Put her down?"

"Yes."

Kevin reluctantly agreed and afterwards went home to tell Elizabeth, who became so hysterical in her grief that she hammered his chest with her fists until he had to hold her hands to protect himself.

"How could you do it?" she cried. "How could you let that woman-hater O'Flaherty kill my dog while my back was turned? It never occurred to you, I suppose, to come home to ask my permission."

She drove to Killage to retrieve the body of the dog, and

then she and John Noonan buried it in the garden at Larch Lawn. She was in a black mood when she returned to Clonglass. She pointedly ignored him and went into the parlour to be alone. After an hour he could stand her absence from the kitchen no longer and he went to her to say that he was sorry.

"The poor creature was in terrible pain and there was no hope of a cure. It seemed the only thing to do."

"You could have waited till you'd asked me."

"I'm sorry."

"If it had been any other vet but O'Flaherty. I can't help thinking than he enjoyed it. One female less in the world."

He sat beside her on the sofa with his arm round her waist, pleased that at least she did not push him away. "You mustn't worry about it now; worry isn't good in your condition."

After a while, to amuse her, he began reading aloud snippets from the local newspaper, and suddenly he burst into laughter. "Listen to this," he said. "It's that ass, the Minister for Agriculture again:

"Brucellosis—Risk of Spread at Calving Time. The Minister of Agriculture, Mr. Liam Hyland, told local farmers at a well-attended meeting at Phelan's Hotel that the greatest danger they faced was not rising taxes but the spread of brucellosis in calving herds.

"'Proper care at calving time,' the Minister said, 'can go a long way towards controlling the spread of the disease, the first essential being to make sure that all calving takes place in isolation from the rest of the herd. It is a fact that cows infected with brucellosis will often not abort but calve normally. These infected animals can spread millions of Brucella organisms when calving and while discharging after calving. As a precaution, all litter, discharges, and after-births should be disinfected and either buried in lime or

159

burnt. These materials should never be put on the manure heap, into the slurry pit, or thrown on waste ground. They could be highly infective and spread disease by contaminating pastures and water supplies.'"

"What's so funny about all that?" Elizabeth asked.

"The Minister makes this speech at least twice a week, as if he knew of nothing else to say. The man is a gowk, like any man who teaches his grandmother to suck eggs."

"Very few farmers could be regarded as his grandmother."

"There's no brucellosis in my herd."

"Pride goeth before destruction, and a haughty spirit before a fall," she said, going to the piano.

The following morning he woke before her, and when he tried to get out of bed he found himself weak at the knees.

"There's something the matter with me," he said. "My legs are weak as water."

"Don't get up then," she said. "I'll fetch the doctor right away."

Ignoring her advice, he tried to dress, but by the time he had put on his shoes he fell back on the bed exhausted. Normally, he enjoyed the rudest of health. He never suffered from anything more serious than the common cold, but now he could hardly believe that he was the same man who took his wife's dog to Killage the previous day.

Dr. Blizzard came in the afternoon, placed a black box of tricks on the stock of the bed, and tapped Kevin's chest and back with delicate fingers. He listened to his heartbeats as if he could hardly hear them, took his pulse and temperature with fearful gravity, and peered into his ears and mouth with the aid of a pencil torch. Waiting for him to give judgement, Kevin watched his sickly yellow face, the creased skin like expensive patent leather, but the doctor kept his mouth firmly shut, as if opening it might invite the entry of untold microbes, disease, maybe death itself.

"Is it flu?" Kevin asked.

"It might be, and then again it might not."

"What could it be?"

"When did it come on?" The doctor ignored his question.

"In the night."

"It came on quickly."

"Could it be the bucko?"

"It could be brucellosis."

"There's no brucellosis in my herd." Kevin laughed sarcastically.

"I've heard that boast before."

"When will you know for certain?"

"I'll have to ask you to come to the hospital for tests."

"And if it's brucellosis, how long will I be laid up?"

"A month, maybe longer."

"It couldn't have happened at a worse time. I'm behind with the hay already."

"If it's brucellosis, hay will be the least of your worries."

Elizabeth drove him to the hospital, where the results of the tests confirmed Blizzard's suspicions. She drove him home and put him to bed in what used to be his father's room, because the doctor at the hospital had told them that brucellosis was infectious. He lay between Elizabeth's green sheets in the stuffy room, bathed in sweat, not knowing the time of day, while notes from a distant piano came up singly through the floorboards. The weather was warm and calm, and outside his neighbours were cutting and baling hay, but that was a remote world, for him a world of sounds rather than sights. Snoddy came up to the bedroom to report after dinner, and Kevin listened with effort and told him to hire what help he needed to get the hay in while it was fine. The

161

world of crops and grazing cattle was far away; all he knew was the sticky sickness lying like thick treacle on his bones, making the smallest movement of a hand or foot exhausting as a mountain trudge. Elizabeth brought him food, but he could not eat, so she brought him orange juice and Bovril, which, in drinking, he spilt on his chest.

He woke up to the barking of Pup, and for a moment he did not know where he was or if it was night or day. He hauled himself up in the bed and leant on his elbow while the running sweat cooled on his neck and chest. Then he knew that he was in the death room, where his father had died and also his mother, and that he could not fall out of bed, because it was deep in the middle like a canoe. Maureen's hearty welcome came up from the kitchen; perhaps Dr. Blizzard had called with another injection and another bottle of tablets. As he listened for an identifiable voice, he relived the moment of waking and his terror as his heart took a sideways plunge. It was an eerily disturbing experience, as if he had been dead and suddenly recalled to life and final judgement. What was most distressing was that his mind was blank as he awoke, as if he had truly been dead, and he wondered if in some pre-posterous way he owed his life to the barking of the dog. He felt as if he'd had a preparative brush with Death. The air in the room was stale and choking like the air in a crypt of cobwebs. He inhaled with his mouth closed, and suddenly the cobwebs were hanging inside his nose. Someone, not Dr. Blizzard, laughed in the kitchen. He felt shaken and insecure, as if neither life nor death was what it seemed.

Exhausted, he fell back in the bed and saw his mother with one frail hand on the banisters coming slowly down the stairs. Shortly after she returned from hospital she came down to dinner, but no sooner had she sat in her chair than the kitchen was filled with a loathsome stink. At first he did not know where it was coming from. It was the foulest smell he had ever experienced, more offensive than the smell of pig shit in an unventilated piggery, or the smell of the decomposed afterbirth that Festus O'Flaherty extracted last year from one of his cows that had failed to cleanse. It was so thick that he felt it blacken the air, falling on his face like a mountain fog until he could almost taste it on his tongue.

"Is that you, Mother?" Maureen asked as she ran to open the window.

"I don't know."

"Well, it isn't me, and I'm sure it isn't Kevin."

"It must be me, then. I can feel the trickle of something warm on my belly."

Maureen ran to the door and retched against the outside wall.

"I don't know where it's coming from," his mother moaned.

"Open your dress and see," Maureen said when she came back to the kitchen. "Come on, Kevin, give her a hand."

Maureen unbuttoned her dress, pulled up her slip, and laid bare the scar on her belly, which had opened in one corner and was discharging a foul brown liquid like farmyard slurry.

Holy Christ! he thought. She's rotting alive in her own house, my own mother, and there isn't a saint in heaven who gives a fuck.

"Stay where you are. Don't get up. I'm going to fetch the doctor right away," he said, glad to escape from the suffocating smell.

"A burst abscess, which should never have been allowed to happen," Dr. Blizzard said and ordered her to hospital, where they inserted a drain to draw off the discharge.

They did not keep her for long, however. They told him that she was incurable, that she would have to go home as soon as the wound healed, because they needed the bed. On her return the pains started in earnest. They came in violent fits that distorted her face and body as she screamed in the rage of pain. Her cries could be heard three fields away, and he dreaded coming back to the house at dinnertime to be reminded of her intolerable suffering.

The flesh melted from her bones. Her face yellowed like a dying leaf, and her head became a case of bone in a cocoon of transparent skin. In her youth she had been big and strong, but never handsome. Now she seemed to him to have taken on the beauty of spirituality as the searing pain burnt away the impurities of the flesh till the flame within her flickered and darted like the flame of a sanctuary lamp in a darkened chapel. But he did not want the spirituality he saw in her because she was at death's door. He wanted her to remain as she was, a big strong woman with a big plain face and hands white from kneading dough in the kitchen. Enraged at the unreason of illness, of life itself, he tackled Dr. Blizzard on his next visit.

"What in the name of God are you giving her?"

"Morphine," the doctor replied, stepping niftily in the dirty yard.

"Well, it's doing her no good. The pain gets worse and worse."

"The longer you take morphine, the more resistant you become to it."

"But she hasn't been taking it long. Can't you give her more?"

"I'm giving her the maximum dose as it is. If I gave her any more, it would kill her."

"Killing would be a mercy," he said fiercely, blocking Blizzard's way so that he could not escape in his car.

"I'm not God, just a doctor."

"God is on holiday, sunning himself in the Canaries. Did you know that, Dr. Blizzard?"

"Life is not mine to confer, nor is it mine to take away."

"I've known vets who showed more mercy to animals in pain than you're showing to my mother."

"I'm doing my duty as a doctor. Don't ask me to do less."

"You look like a man about to quote the Hippocritic Oath."

"Hippocratic, Mr. Hurley, Hippocratic. And now, if you don't mind, I've got another call to make."

"Pompous fucker," Kevin shouted after him as he vanished through the first gate of the lane.

He came back from the field that evening to find his mother crying out again. Maureen had gone shopping and his father was lying on his back in the next room with cotton plugs in his ears. He went into her room and stood by the window unable to look at the twisted face. She reached for his hand and motioned him to sit on the edge of the bed.

"Won't some of ye put me out of my misery?" she implored with what breath she could find between gasps.

Without a word, he lifted her in the bed and put the pillow between her face and his chest. Then he pressed her face against the pillow and held her like a lover, tightly against his body, until her futile struggle stopped. When she was quiet, he laid her gently on the bed and folded her arms over her stomach.

Beneath the window were two apple trees and the apples were glowing in the evening sun. He looked down on their red and yellow cheeks and the sparrow droppings like calcified white worms on the ones near the wall where the birds roosted in the branches. He had once heard Festus say that in America farmers fed dried poultry droppings to beef cattle.

Maureen was coming up the lane with bicycle and shopping bag. It was the fifth of October, he was in his thirty-seventh year, and his mother would never feel pain again.

Lying now on the bed she died in, he was closer to her than he'd ever been in life. It was as if she were standing by the curtain in the thickening dusk. A tear trickled down his cheek. He heard steps on the stairs and he hid his face in the sheet.

"And how is our patient today?" Monsignor McGladdery asked from the door. As a parish priest was the last man he wished to see, Kevin wondered about the best way to discourage him.

"It's a shame to be lying up here, and all the work that's to be done in the fields."

"That's good Christian thinking, my son. As the Pope himself said while he was here, Love the work of the fields, for it keeps you close to God, the Creator, in a special way. But you must wish for recovery only in moderation, you must not despair. God sends us these trials only to test our love for him. Think of Job. I know that you are a man, born of a woman and therefore full of misery, that in the span of a year you have lost your father, your nephew, and your best friend; but what's happened to you is nothing compared with what befell poor Job. Now, repeat after me: 'The Lord gave and the Lord hath taken away; blessed be the name of the Lord.'"

"I'm too weak to pray." He closed his eyes.

The Monsignor came to the bedside and took his wrist to feel his pulse. He was a tall broad-shouldered man in his mid-sixties, with unruly white hair that stood out in tufts from the sides of his big round head like lengths of thirteen-amp fuse wire. He never wore a suit, always a black cassock with a wide shiny seat, and though he was straight in the back, he leant forward at an angle of seventy-five degrees as he walked. For that reason, if no other, he had captured the imagination of his parishioners, the most devout of whom believed that it was only the strength of his faith, not his sense of balance, that kept him from falling flat on his face.

In his youth he was famous above all for his love of boiled bacon and cabbage. He was then much given to visiting farmhouses before dinnertime and supervising the cooking of the bacon, in return for which he expected to sit down at table with his host. Though he spent much time alone with women in kitchens, their husbands trusted him implicitly, believing as they did that harmless eccentricity is a certain hallmark of a celibate clergy. In recent years, however, he had to forgo his favourite dish because of high blood pressure. Dr. Blizzard told him that he must not touch salty foods, that on no account must he eat boiled bacon, that he must not even eat cabbage that had been boiled in the same water as bacon. The doctor's interdict was a severe trial to him, but he submitted to it scrupulously except on Christmas Day, when he scorned turkey and goose and enjoyed a heaped plate of fine red bacon and the firm white heart of a cabbage with plenty of tomato chutney.

During the rest of the year, he contented himself with collecting the string that is used to bind bacon in the pot. He would often enter farmhouses and demand bacon string, which he would then secrete in a watertight tobacco pouch that he carried for the purpose. Many were the theorists among his flock who speculated on the destination of the string, but most adhered to one of two schools of thought—those who believed that he chewed it in the privacy of his parlour and those who argued that he put it in his pipe and smoked it. Kevin belonged to neither school. He believed, though he never revealed his belief, that the string absorbed some of the carcinogenic agent from the bacon, and that the

Monsignor was sufficiently saintly to collect the string for the protection of his less well-informed parishioners.

"We often forget that God never closes one door without opening another," the Monsignor continued, sitting on the edge of the bed.

Sacred Heart of Jesus, for mercy's sake take him away, Kevin echoed Maureen's heartfelt prayer.

"When Dr. Blizzard found that I had high blood pressure and decided to deny me bacon, I thought at first that life wouldn't be worth living. But I hadn't reckoned on God's ingenuity in the land of darkness and the shadow of death, because I soon discovered that the pleasure of having your blood pressure taken is greater than the pleasure of eating bacon and cabbage."

"Ah, go 'way!"

"It's a strange thought, I admit. I've discussed it with many patients, but I've still to meet the man who enjoys the sphygmomanometer as I do. Have you ever seen a sphygmomanometer?" he asked enthusiastically.

"No," said Kevin, twisting in the bed with impatience.

"It's a strange yoke doctors have for taking the blood pressure. It's got a pneumatic cuff you wrap round your biceps, but if you haven't got an arm, you can wrap it round your thigh just as easily. The doctor keeps his finger on your pulse while pumping up the cuff until the pulse can no longer be felt. Now, it's in this pumping action that my pleasure lies, so much so that I drove up to Dublin a few months ago and bought my own sphygmomanometer. If you like, I'll bring it along tomorrow and take your blood pressure so that you'll see what I mean."

"There's nothing wrong with my blood pressure."

Ignoring him, the Monsignor launched on a meandering discourse on systolic and diastolic pressure and the reason why he wore galoshes even in the middle of summer. The next thing Kevin knew was that he was being shaken by the shoulder.

"You *are* weak, by Jude. You fell asleep right in the middle of my conversation. Now, the reason I came was to bring you viaticum, food for the journey."

"What journey?"

"The journey into the world to come. But in your case it's to help you get better."

"The only journey I'm going to make is a journey to Roscrea in three weeks to give a lecture on foggage."

"Of course, you'll have to make your confession first." The Monsignor kissed his ribbonlike stole and put it round his neck.

"I'm not ready to make my confession," Kevin said in alarm.

He went to confession only once a year, at Easter, and then he went to the monks in Roscrea, where he wasn't known. He did not trust the Monsignor. Perhaps Maureen had confessed her incest, and the Monsignor had come because he knew all about him. Maureen went to confession once a month, but surely she must have found some way of calling a spade an agricultural implement. She wouldn't dare tell the priest that she was having it off with her brother. He looked up at the Monsignor and imagined his voice raised in weary admonition:

A terrible sin, worse than masturbation, my son. In masturbation you are only destroying your own soul, but in incest, as in all fornication, you are pulling another soul down with you. Even if you find the grace and strength to give up your sin, how do you know that your partner will be able to do the same?

The Monsignor suddenly changed tack. "I remember ten years ago I used to visit an old man who lived over in Derrycon. We used to sit by the fire while the bacon and cabbage boiled in the pot, and then after a good yarn and a good dinner the old man would come and kneel beside me and say 'Bless me, Father, for I have sinned,' as if confession after bacon and cabbage was like sunshine after a shower. He was a walking saint, that old man. When he died, he went straight to heaven. God never tested him, because he did not need testing. But you are being tested, and if I were you, I wouldn't turn my back on the chance to ease my conscience. You may not see yourself as a sinner, but in spite of what the theologians say, I'm convinced that a man can sin without knowing it, because sin is in his heart, in the baseness of his nature. What could be more natural than what Satan was doing in the Book of Job—going to and fro in the earth, and walking up and down in it—but, because it was Satan who was walking, it was sinful. I'm not saying that you are a man of sin, but you are a sinful man. If nothing else, you've been going to and fro in the earth, and walking up and down in it. So, now will you make your confession?"

"I'll make my confession when I'm ready to make it. Now all I'm ready for is sleep."

"Take care that you remember to wake up."

The Monsignor put his stole in his pocket and hurried out of the room at the highly precarious angle of sixty-five degrees. Outside the window, the green of treetops rose above the sill and behind them a sky of unnatural blue with a becalmed white cloud in the centre. The weakness ran like thin liquid through his bones, and he closed his eyes, subdued by pain and the scornful phantoms that fled like spots before his eyes. When he woke, the day had changed. The green of the treetops had darkened and the white cloud had been replaced by a formless field of grey. He felt shaken and insecure. In this canoe of a bed, anything, even death itself, was possible. It was as if his tractors had been weapons of war, that without them he was a defenceless waif. He shivered under the clothes, not from cold but from the degradation of life's infirmities. He banged on the floor with a mug in the hope that Elizabeth would hear, but the clomping tread on the stairs told him that it was Maureen who was coming to his aid.

"Where's Elizabeth?" he asked.

"She's gone to Killage or Larch Lawn. She didn't say which."

"Will you make me a cup of tea propped up with a dash of whiskey?"

"You're beginning to sound like His Dotage, may he rest. I noticed the Monsignor left in a rush."

"Have you been confessing to him lately?"

"You know I do the First Fridays."

"Have you told him about us?"

"No."

"And how can you go to confession without confessing your biggest sin?"

"I'm treating it as a reserved sin."

"What do you mean?"

"A sin to be confessed to a bishop."

"But you don't know any bishops!"

"Then, I'll wait till I do."

"Oh, go and make my tea, you mad woman, and don't aggravate my illness with your capers."

Dr. Blizzard came in the morning and gave him an injection in the thigh. After he left, Kevin lay on his back stewing in sweat, recalling the acrid stench that used to rise from the mare's back when he took off the straddle after coming from the bog. Now he felt nearer the mare than his tractors. Snoddy was at the farthest end of the earth, and Elizabeth and Maureen no longer pestered him with their nocturnal claims. Sickness, while tethering him to the bedpost, had freed him from the slow attrition of their demands. He tried

171

to move to a cooler place in the bed, but kept sinking back into the middle, pursued by pain. After a while he got up to go to the toilet, and as he looked out of the little window, he spied Billy Snoddy following Maureen into the yard. He crossed the landing to Elizabeth's room to get a better look, but by the time he got there they had vanished from view. Where had they gone? Into the dairy? Into the stable? Or up into the hay shed? Had he really seen them or had he imagined it all?

As he stood by the bedside table, his hand touched a red-covered book. It was a diary, Elizabeth's diary, written in black ink in a small stubborn hand. He did not know if he should read it, but before he had time to decide he was half-way down the page.

August 20th
I saw a television programme about black holes in space that can swallow up whole planets. Does Kevin see women as black holes into which an unwary man might vanish without trace? I have learnt that he fears women, thanks to O'Flaherty. He told me that once he thought a woman's natural juices were acid, like the stagnant water in sour bogs, and that he lived in fear of the corrosive effect they might have on his member. I hope that I have days to prove to him that women are exquisite; gentle and selfless as well as fair; that the much-feared vagina is a chamber for the performance of the most heavenly string music, not a dangerous tumulus full of sharp-edged potsherds; that it entices and enfolds rather than maims; that the invitation to sexual congress is as innocent as an invitation to afternoon tea (Another cup, Monsignor?), not an occasion for forced entry and robbery under arms.

August 26th
Today I was lying in Rowan's Field reading Herrick, when I

heard the word "Kevin" from the other side of the hedge. I listened hard as the voices drew nearer, and I realized that I was listening to Maureen and Snoddy.

"If you don't do it, I'll tell the quare one," Snoddy threatened.

"What will you tell her?" Maureen asked.

"About you and Kevin."

"There's nothing to tell that she can't guess."

"Now, don't give me that. I caught you red-handed, flagrante delicto as the lawyers say."

"If you as much as breathed a word, Kevin would fling your stones to the crows. Have you thought of that?"

Their voices faded as they walked away and though I listened I could hear no more. I am obviously the quare one, but what secret is there between Kevin and Maureen that I should guess but must not hear? And what did he want Maureen to do that might occasion the stoning of crows? I suppose I should ask Kevin, but he might be shocked at my suspicions. He is such an obviously good and simple man, the kind of man through whom the binding agent of civilization is bequeathed.

He no longer felt three removes from life; the worlds of Maureen, Snoddy, and Elizabeth came spilling like a cataract into the bedroom. He took the diary back to his room and read it from start to finish. Elizabeth's world was rarefied, full of dreams and music and observations that had never before been made at Clonglass. He was flattered to discover that she saw him as simple and good, incapable of deception, a man whose only fault must really count in her romantic eyes as virtue—his preference for the loud trombone as opposed to heavenly string music in bed. It seemed impossible that such a woman should sit at the same table and breathe the same air as Snoddy.

Maureen came up with his tea at four.

"Where is the Abominable Ruminant?" he asked.

"Bringing in the last of the bales. I've never seen a man work so hard without a ganger."

"He's no innocent. If he threatens you, let me know."

"Why should he threaten me?"

"He might threaten to tell Elizabeth about you and me unless you lie with him."

"The brucellosis is giving you strange ideas. It's not good for you to lie in bed with it alone."

He studied her big face, but she was laughing at him, giving nothing of herself away.

"I'm powerless now, but I won't be powerless for long. Snoddy may try something while I'm low, but hold him off for a week or two. Tell him anything that will keep him quiet, but don't give in to him. If he lays a hand on you, I'll horsewhip him within an inch of his life, and when I've horsewhipped him I'll put him lying flat on a bogey and drive two six-inch nails through his briefcase."

"Do you want me to tell him that?"

"No, I'll tell him."

"Then, why did you tell me?"

"I only wanted you to know my thoughts."

Elizabeth came and read to him in the evening, but though he heard the words they did not make sentences. All he could think of was the purity of her heart and the far from remote possibility that he might lose her. He knew from her diary that her idea of him was so divorced from the reality of his life that if she discovered the murky truth she would never again share a house let alone a bed with him. He closed his eyes, pretending to be asleep, and she closed her book and kissed his forehead before going down the stairs.

Slowly, the pain ebbed from his bones and the beginnings of strength returned. He got up for an hour or two and walked in the yard in a heavy overcoat, but after twenty minutes he realized that Snoddy could knock him down by breathing on the back of his neck. He decided to go back to bed, to conserve his strength for his lecture to the Roscrea Macra.

"You're not going to Roscrea in your present condition to talk about foggage," Elizabeth told him that evening. "The very look of you would frighten an ass from his oats."

"But the Macra asked me months ago, and I'm not going to let them down. I know the subject arseways. All I need is to get there."

"Well, you're not driving to Roscrea by yourself."

"I was expecting you to take me."

"I have more to do than spend an evening in a bare hall watching you riding your favourite hobbyhorse."

"I'll get Festus to drive me, then."

"No, you won't. I don't want you out drinking with that overgrown schoolboy. If you must get there, I'll drive you myself."

That settled that. He was still weak and shivery on the evening, but he felt it his duty to propagate the Foggage Principle in a land of devil may care. He was a faint beacon in the mists of indifference, but in years to come he would be remembered for his foresight, and to be going on with, there would be a picture of Elizabeth and himself in the next *Farmers' Journal*.

They arrived in Roscrea on a warm evening of mist and rain, and as they were early he first had a drink to steady his nerves. When they got to the hall, he was disappointed at the poor turnout, but when he saw Festus O'Flaherty in the front seat flanked by the widow from Clonaslew, he took heart. He was glad of Festus, not merely for the sake of his companionship but because he now knew that no matter what went wrong he had audience.

The chairman made a short speech of introduction,

which Kevin was too distracted to hear. He felt shaky and uncertain, and he could see that Elizabeth was not herself. She was sitting alone on the end of a bench, smoking a cigarette through her long black holder, a certain sign of unease. He began his talk with a definition of "foggage" and took a sip from the glass of water provided for his convenience.

"What I want you to take home with you this evening," he continued, "is the knowledge that foggage is conserved grass, and that grass, which is the cheapest food, is milk and meat. Therefore, any means of extending the grazing season and shortening the period of stall-feeding is a boon to the farmer. And that is what the Foggage Principle is about—the extension of the grazing season by grass management into late autumn and winter so that the farmer can rely less on hay, silage, and supplementary feed. But if we are to make grass available to cattle in the form of foggage well into December, or even into January, we must be prepared . . ."

While he was still only warming to his subject, a drunken voice from the back of the hall shouted, "Fuck foggage!" What he had taken to be a heap of old coats rose up in the form of a tall brutal-looking man. If he had been in good health, he would not have minded the interruption, but he hesitated in mid-sentence while everyone in the hall looked round.

"Fuck foggage!" the man said again, as if he had discovered the *mot juste* and was sticking to it. "You're a false prophet. You're deluding the Macra, who are too young to know better. The Irish climate is too wet for late winter grazing. Think, dear Macra, of the effect of animals' hooves on the sward and the soil structure. You're off your pinhead, Hurley. Every farmer with a milligram of sense knows that in this country you must take your cattle off the land by November to give spring grass a chance to grow. Even your grandmother would tell you that you can't have your grass and eat it. The foggage man pays the price of his fogology in a late spring the following year. So I say, my dear Macra, 'Fuck foggage and all fucking fogologists!'"

Just then Festus got up from his seat, drew a copper ring from his pocket, and held it up for all to see.

"I've got a self-piercing bull ring here," he said, "and if you don't fog off this minute I'll drive it through your nose and lead you from this hall like a suckling lamb on my little finger. I'll give you thirty seconds to make a move."

The man gathered his raincoat round him and left without another word. Festus sat down, said a word in the widow's ear, and resumed his torpedo-shaped cigar. The rest of the talk passed without incident, ending with questions and enthusiastic applause.

"You did well," Elizabeth said, taking his arm.

"I'm dying for a pint," he said with relief.

"I want to go home."

"We'll just have the one."

"If there's one thing I can't stand, it's smoky pubs and the smell of spilt stout." Elizabeth looked adamant.

"We'll go to the hotel, then," said Festus, who had just joined them. "It's only ten yards up the street."

Reluctantly, she went with them, but only because Kevin was parched after his talk.

The hotel lounge was an empty cavern of dim lights, and they stood by the bar, wondering where to sit, while Festus ordered.

"I'll have a pink gin," said the widow. "And tell him I like the pink in."

"I didn't for a moment expect you to prefer it out," said Festus.

Kevin began telling Elizabeth about an even more sombre hotel in case she should spot the double entendre, but he could tell from the tilt of her nose that the damage had already been done. They took their drinks to a corner while Festus began recounting a case of incest between father and daughter which he had read about in the English papers.

The widow listened as if his every word was meat and spirituous drink. She had dark hair, dark eyes, and a dark complexion, with a dark mole on her left cheek. Her lips were dark red, as if stained by claret, and her fingernails were painted the colour of peonies. Yet in spite of the overall darkness, she glittered like a dewdrop in the sun. Her middle-aged neck supported a flashing necklace, her smile revealed two gold teeth, and her fingers twinkled with sentimentally valuable rings. What Kevin was most aware of, however, was the prominence of what Festus called her "iliac crests" and the way she discharged the scent of valerian whenever she moved her bangled wrists. He looked at Elizabeth to find contemptuous disapproval written plainly on her uncompromising chin.

"The father was in the habit of masturbating his daughter with a sausage," Festus said. "And once when she had finished, he ate the sausage."

"What did she say to that?" The widow fluttered dark overlong eyelashes.

"How can you, Daddy? How can you eat a sausage without cooking it?" Festus mimicked.

"I wonder why he ate it," the widow pursued.

"He may have missed lunch," said Festus.

"Enough is enough," said Elizabeth, getting up. "Come on, Kevin, we're for the road."

"Can't you wait till I finish my drink?" he said.

"I'll wait outside in the car."

"You too have domesticated a tigress," Festus said when she had gone.

"You didn't rush," Elizabeth told him in the car.

"You forget that Festus is my friend."

"If he were your friend, he'd have some respect for your wife. He's little better than a savage. He denies the first law of civilization—the acceptance of women."

She drove in sullen silence until they were a mile from home. Then she said without turning to look at him, "Life at Clonglass is impossible. If you don't get rid of Maureen and Snoddy, I'm going to return to Larch Lawn. It's the obvious place for us to live, a big comfortable house away from the chafing of mean and disgusting natures."

"Give me a day or so to get back on my feet," he replied, wondering how long he could put off the day of reckoning.

10

Kevin did not get up the following day. He had a relapse, and like any wife who never misses a trick, Elizabeth predicted it.

"A man who preaches the conservation of grass should first consider the conservation of his strength," she told him as she brought him his mid-morning Bovril.

Dr. Blizzard came after lunch, chided him for getting up from his sickbed without permission, diagnosed pleurisy, and forecast a further month in bed for him.

Kevin's sickness was a sore trial to Elizabeth. Left to cope with Maureen and Snoddy alone, she found that their coarseness at table was too much for her. She spent most of her time in the parlour, and rarely if ever even ate in the kitchen. The grey blotches between her toes had spread, filling her with a sense of fragility and self-loathing.

"I'm sure it's the house," she told Dr. Blizzard. "I had a perfectly healthy dog, a big Labrador, that went down with an allergy within a month of moving to Clonglass."

"I'm sorry I don't follow," said the ladylike Blizzard, his back forming a perfect curve as he stooped over her feet.

"It's because I've moved house. Though I don't like saying so, it isn't as clean as the house I've been used to. Hence the allergy."

"Very unlikely. Allergies, you see, are commonest in hygienic environments. Asthma and hay fever are almost unknown in primitive societies. In other words, the more parasites, the less chance of allergy."

"What is it, then?"

"You have a foot fungus, nothing very serious. We'll have you right in next to no time."

"What are you going to give me for it?"

"Tablets."

"Antihistamine?"

"Certainly not."

"That's what the vet gave my Labrador."

"But you're not suffering from an allergy."

"What kind of tablets?"

"Now, don't worry your pretty little head, my dear. Just take them three times a day and watch the blotches disappear."

After two weeks the blotches had got worse. They also appeared on her hands, and her fingernails thickened and changed colour.

"It isn't a foot fungus," Dr. Blizzard said when she went back to him.

"Is it a hand fungus?" she asked sarcastically.

"I fear I've been treating you for the wrong disease. You are suffering from psoriasis, my dear."

"Are you sure it isn't an allergy?"

"Certain."

"Can you cure it?"

"No, there is no cure for psoriasis. All that medicine can

do is to minimize the effects. I can only prescribe sunlight and tar ointment."

She drove up to Dublin the following day to see a specialist. He examined her feet and hands and told her that she was host to a fungus with which he would deal very expeditiously. He gave her a prescription she could not read, but, when she presented it to a chemist, she received a bottle of the tablets that Blizzard first prescribed for her. She threw the tablets in the Liffey and made several telephone calls until she found another specialist who could see her at short notice. When she told him about the conflicting diagnoses, he replied that he would quickly end the conflict by taking a scraping for analysis and that he would get in touch with her before the weekend with his definitive findings. His finding was that she was suffering from psoriasis, and he too prescribed sunlight and a tar preparation.

On a Saturday morning she went out to the yard to expose herself to sun and fresh air. Henry had come out of his loose box to look at her over the bars. Since Kevin had taken to his bed, Snoddy had been stall-feeding him, too afraid to lead him out to graze. He was a noble prisoner, perhaps a kindred spirit. She recalled that in her first weeks at Clonglass she used to go out to the field where he was tethered and listen to the tearing sound the grass made as he pulled. He was alert, almost fearsome, always ready for aggression, unlike his tame castrated sons in the next field. She wondered if he would ever come to know her well enough to trust her. If he should come to the gate where she stood, she would reach out a gentling hand and touch his wrinkled dewlap. But gentling was not for him. His pander had put a ring in his nose so that he could lead him to whichever heifer he pleased. Now his life was entirely devoted to service. A reputable butcher would not look twice at his tough and sinewy flesh. All he possessed was his hide and oft-proved prepotency.

She walked across Rowan's Field to a larger field with three young oaks beyond. Under each tree was a jungle of tall nettles, and she could not help wondering why the cattle had not trampled them when they were small. They must have wished to shelter under the trees from time to time, but perhaps the nettles had grown while they were grazing other fields. It was early morning, and the grass was still too wet to lie on, so she chose an upturned bogey in a corner and stretched her legs in the life-giving sun. Beyond the hedge was another hedge and another hedge, and somewhere in the distance were the changing blues and greens of Slieve Bloom. She could not see it at will in her mind's eye. It was a day of white clouds, limbless monsters crawling on their bellies, crowding together like angry buffalo, blotting out the sun for minutes at a time. Now the field was in shadow, and half of Slieve Bloom would frown while the other half smiled in the changing light.

Her eye rested on eleven of Kevin's cows at the far end of the field, and she thought idly that she was looking at the loveliest of all midland scenes—cows chewing the cud in a field, lying with their heads up, their forelegs folded and their tails tucked away, their smooth backs and rumps curving to the ground. They were facing in different directions, some looking at one another, some back to back, some side by side; and yet there was an inevitability in their positions as if they had been posed by a supreme painter.

The sun warmed her feet and she closed her eyes to find the hedges rushing up to jostle her. Life, she felt, had robbed her of experience in its proper season. She had spent her girlhood in a convent and her early womanhood in a Dublin bed-sitter, so that when she came to her husband she was incapable of throwing the ballast of the past overboard and sailing before the wind without looking astern. In her lack of experience she had fallen under the spell of an empty youth which was now in danger of becoming an empty middle age. Her fear now was that she would die before she saw life plain, before reaching maturity and unhurried objectivity, before learning to enjoy lark song as much as "The Lark Ascending." If only she could do something inexplicable, or at least something she herself could not explain, something truly surprising like composing an étude for the piano. It would be a means of escape from the limitations of the conscious life, of allowing darkness expression, of transcending the maze of fields and hedges that hemmed her in.

She had been lonely after Murt's death, and now she was still alone, her isolation expressed in the self-loathing she felt when she looked at the lesions on her hands and feet, a disgusting leprosy that forced her to wear gloves to church and to the shops, that made her envy even Maureen and Billy Snoddy. She had been born with a sense of her own beauty, an awareness of the desirability of her body, but now her body was not her own. She had become host to a parasite, and Blizzard had told her that there was a one-in-ten chance that her baby would come into the same inheritance. She turned her head away from the sun in disgust as she saw a baby girl with a blotchy face, ugly and grey.

Impatiently, as if trying to escape, she walked down the field, veering towards the lane so as not to disturb the ruminating cows. The two that were standing followed her slowly, then eyed each other vacuously as she vanished through the gate. All round her was the wreckage of rusty machinery peering out of grass and nettles—an old cultivator, an old plough, a disc harrow, the cutter bar of a mower, a seed hopper with a dent. Henry was still looking over the bars, staling on a half-eaten turnip, a Friesian bull with a white scrotum, heavy and smooth, not wrinkled and shrivelled like his master's. Yet it wasn't absolutely smooth; you could just discern the outline of the two stones inside it. He was looking at her bare white legs as if she were a Friesian heifer, unaware of her psoriasis, and she felt as if she had glided through the closed gate, touched the great warm valise, and felt the weight of it in her hand.

I'm going mad, she told herself. Slowly but surely, I'm losing my reason.

Pup came up behind and sniffed her calves, then poked his nose up her skirt as if he expected her to be in heat. She turned sharply and pushed him away with her shoe.

"It's strange how that dog's always sniffing your legs," Maureen said from the door of the shed.

"It's stranger how he never sniffs yours," Snoddy joked in the darkness behind her.

"Ach, sure he's used to mine. He's known them since he was a month."

"Or maybe he's just partial to a whiff of the water of Cologne." Snoddy laughed.

Ignoring them, Elizabeth went into the house for her purse. The lowness of their conversation had reinforced her sense of defilement. She felt that she must escape, and one way to escape was to do the weekend shopping in Killage.

As a little treat, she decided to take the Mercedes. She had a car of her own, a new Mini, but now that Kevin was out of circulation she enjoyed nothing better than driving his dirty Mercedes. In fact, it was one of the few things at Clonglass that she liked better than her own possessions at Larch Lawn. When she had done the shopping, she put the bag on the back seat and said a prayer for her unborn baby in the musty church. Then she remembered that she must call at Larch Lawn for some sheet music, and she brightened at the thought of sitting for ten minutes in the parlour while she sipped a dry sherry and listened to the emptiness of the house.

The men were in the fields, the farmyard empty except for a low trailer. She wandered from room to room, asking herself how she could conceivably have left, and then she sat with her sherry, looking out at the soothingly familiar scene.

"You have a very fluidic personality," he told her across the table. "Almost pantomorphic, I should say."

They were sitting in the hotel lounge, looking across the road and the valley to the Glen of the Downs, and beyond the wooded slopes on either side were six fields, gold and green, near the horizon. It was a sunlit Sunday morning, and she drank three schooners of dry sherry and wished that lunchtime would never come.

"You have a fluidic personality," he repeated, and she wondered if all Englishmen spoke his lingo or if it were only technical journalists.

"If you're not hungry, I'll cook you lunch," she said.

"How very Irish! Now what would you cook me if I were starving?"

"A pantomorphic pastry."

"But what did you mean?"

He had auburn hair and a walrus moustache that made her wish to touch the corners of it with her cheek, and when he laughed he revealed an arc of ivory-perfect teeth and closed his sea-blue eyes.

"I meant that I have nothing planned. Lunch will take a long time to prepare, too long perhaps for a hungry man."

"I must plead a previous engagement. I must look up a friend in Arklow, but I shall come back to take you out again this evening."

They returned to the hotel at seven and sat at the same table by the window. The slopes of the Glen were now a dark green, and on the horizon was a pool of sky beneath a thunder cloud. In the reflected evening light the six fields, gold and green, had melted into what looked like a flat and fishless sea, and she felt that at any moment a white yacht would heave in sight between the sombre slopes.

"The Glen looks thickly wooded from here," she said.

"In the distance it is a carpet of green but on the nearer slopes you can make out the shapes of individual trees. What do they remind you of?" he asked.

"Big green cauliflowers."

"No, you are wrong. They are like monstrous heads of broccoli. 'Tis broccoli lends enchantment to the view, or words to that effect."

She could not get a word of sense out of him all evening, nothing but conventional phrases turned inside out to look like new and fag ends of quotations that teased her memory of old advertisements and poems from her school anthology. His moustache, however, lent enchantment to his views, and she could see the hungry eyes of older women turning to their table, to the slopes of the Glen, and back to Alexander Utley.

As Attracta had gone down the country for the weekend, she invited him back to the bed-sitter for a cup of Algerian coffee and a large digestive biscuit. The coffee and the biscuit made him dull. He fell asleep on the settee, and when she woke him at twelve he asked if he could stay the night.

"No need for a bed. I'll camp right here," he said.

"There are two beds, and you can have one of them."

She decided to let him have her own bed. The thought of his naked legs stretching luxuriously between her sheets would provide celibate titillation as she herself curled up under Attracta's freesia-laden duvet. She woke in the dark centre of the night to find him naked beside her, his hand already on her breasts, his moustache tickling her cheek. She moved

187

in a dream, the duvet slipped to the floor, but he kept the cool night air from her body and whispered in her ear at the end, "Have you ever seen the inside of a tumulus?

"It's an ancient burial mound," he said when she failed to reply. "That's what you're like inside, a narrow entrance followed by a narrow corridor with a wide central chamber beyond."

Tears welled in her eyes and ran between her lids but she did not speak. She lay weeping on the bed while he made thumping noises in the next room, and when she woke in the morning he had already gone. She never saw him again, but she would never forget him, nor her callowness, her naiveté, her soon-to-be slaughtered innocence.

She sorted out some sheet music and returned to the car to find Pup sitting on the back seat chewing the pork steak she had just bought and a torn packet of biscuits beside him. He had hidden in the back unbeknown to her, and now he was so pleased to see her that he darted out and sniffed her knees and thighs. Looking round to see if anyone was watching, she went into the shed for a length of rope. She dropped the rope on the front seat beside her, and Pup jumped in and sat on it. When she was halfway home, she backed the car into a laneway and set off smartly between the overhanging trees in the direction of the Grove. When she came to the Tree House, she tied a noose on one end of the rope and flung it over a branch above her head. Pup was circling round her, trying to lick her hands and legs, making silly supplicating noises, but she slipped the noose down over his ears, tightened it, and pulled the other end to hoist him off the ground. He made a few pathetic attempts to scratch at the rope with his forepaws as she tied the loose end to a lower branch, and she turned away because it would not have been civilized to look. She had seen a dog hanged once before. She had seen her father hang a stray collie that had been stealing eggs.

With an absence of guilt that surprised her, she drove back to Killage for more pork steak and arrived home about noon, feeling in need of another sherry. Absent-mindedly, she opened the door of the dairy to put the pork in the freezer, and the first thing she took in was Billy Snoddy winking at her. It was only after she had recoiled from the devilishness in his eye that she saw clearly what he was doing. Maureen was bending over a tub with her skirt draped over her head, and Snoddy was standing behind her, enjoying her final, or at least her penultimate, favours. She closed the door before he had time to smile at her, hurried into the house, and put the meat in the fridge.

After drinking a schooner of sherry at a draught, she ran upstairs to tell Kevin, but when she saw him sitting up in bed absorbed in one of Murt's books, she wondered if what she had seemed to see had really happened.

"What are you reading?" she asked, for something natural to say.

"A paper on piss: 'The effects of urine and its components on the botanical composition and production of a grass/clover sward.'"

"If Murt was alive, you could talk to him about it."

"If you make me a cup of tea, I'll talk to you about it."

She smoothed the coverlet and kissed his cheek. Then she took her diary from her bedroom and sat for a long time at the parlour table with pen poised as if she could not bring herself to write. At last she began, her hand moving slowly across the page as if the choice of words were important:

I can barely believe what I have just seen in the dairy, Billy Snoddy copulating with Maureen as she stooped over a tub of molassed beet pulp. He had gripped her round the waist with both hands, and he was bending at the knees, in and out, in and out, like a deranged trombonist in a Bruckner symphony. I was so frightened that I did not look a second time, did not look to see if he had possessed her *per anum* or *per cunnum*. Strange how I can write those words in Latin but not in Anglo-Saxon, they are so coarse. But how can I think such thoughts and remain a good-living woman, going to Mass and the sacraments, the First Fridays and rosary and benediction? Perhaps God, not the devil, sends me these thoughts so that I can triumph over temptation for his greater glory. I am certain that the greatest saints had disgusting thoughts, that their sainthood resided in the moral value of their struggle against them. The greatest sinners, someone must surely have said, are potentially the greatest saints. But perhaps I delude myself, refusing to see that in living with Maureen and Snoddy I have become one of them. The thoughts I had about Henry this morning could have been Maureen's, they were so lewd. I wouldn't have had them a year ago. And then what I did to Pup was done by a "me" I've never known before. If I allow myself to drift, shall I too find myself in the dairy with Snoddy? Are all human beings more similar than dissimilar? Now that I've put it on paper, I know what to do.

"I've just caught Maureen and Snoddy in the dairy," she told Kevin as she handed him his tea.

"What were they doing?"

"They were behaving as if they were married. But it wasn't the doing of it that startled me, it was the way they were doing it—like animals from behind. Two sins in one, as if one were not enough. To add insult to injury, he winked and looked at me like a mad trombonist who was dissatisfied with the number of positions on his slide."

"He should have been out at the hay on a fine day like this."

"Is that all you've got to say?"

"What do you expect me to say?"

"I expect you to call him up here and sack him on the spot."

"But I can't sack him till I get well. Who would look after the place? You and Maureen?"

"Goodbye."

"Where are you going?"

"Back to Larch Lawn. I refuse to be humiliated further in what should be my own house."

"Be reasonable, Elizabeth. Wait for a week or two till I get my strength back."

"I can't make up my mind if you're too good for this world or just too weak. I'll come back to cook for you every day, but I'm not sleeping another night under the same roof as Maureen and Snoddy."

She had made up her mind. She went straight to her bedroom and began packing her things.

11

The day after Elizabeth left for Larch Lawn, Festus came to see him. Grey and careworn, he sat on the edge of the bed and told Kevin that the tigress had brought an injunction against him, prohibiting him from entering the house on the grounds that he was violent and abusive.

"She didn't even tell me that she was contemplating legal action. She brought me my breakfast in bed with a letter from her solicitor on the tray. After twenty years of marriage and four children, she had as much consideration for me as she would for a worm. But I didn't allow her to see that I was hurt. I laughed in her face, packed a suitcase, and set off for Clonaslew and the Widow Heaviside. When I told her my story, she laughed in *my* face and told me not to be silly, to go back to my wife where I belonged. She was horrified at my suggestion that I should share her house. Her house was her own, she said, and one 'husband' enough in a lifetime."

"Well, you've always said that you knew your women." Kevin smiled.

"But in my wildest fantasies I wouldn't have foreseen this. Now I have nowhere to live. I'm staying at Phelan's, but I can't live forever in a hotel. I was wondering if you would let me have Larch Lawn for six months till I've had time to look round."

"Elizabeth is staying at Larch Lawn. She moved back there yesterday."

"For good?"

"Who can tell?"

"You can put me up here, then. I'm no trouble. All I need is a room. Anything would be better than a hotel."

"I'm afraid I can't help. I'm trying to get Elizabeth to come back, you see. She'd never return if you were here."

"You hard-hearted bastard."

"I'm sorry, Festus, but there it is. And anyhow Larch Lawn isn't mine to give away."

"I wasn't asking you to give it away. I'm willing to pay rent."

"You look as if you could do with a drink."

"I have a pain like a knife in my guts. I haven't had a wink of sleep for a week. What I need is somewhere quiet for a month or two."

"What about Lalor's. It's empty, isn't it?"

"That's all I get wherever I turn. Suggestions galore and never a helping hand."

"In my present state there's nothing I can do for you."

"Goodbye, then, and may the devil protect you from warble fly, balanitis, pizzle rot, and the white scour, you ungrateful bugger."

He closed the bedroom door, his shoulders stooped under the weight of self-pity. For a moment Kevin sensed O'Flaherty's helplessness in his bones before returning to the subject that occupied him most—Maureen and Billy Snoddy. Snoddy came up to the bedroom every day to report to him as he himself used to report to his father before he became a dotard. Maureen brought him tea and made a string of none too subtle jokes about the Lady of Larch Lawn. Contrary to his inclination, he maintained an inscrutable silence with them both, knowing that he would need all his strength to confront Snoddy and that if he challenged Maureen now she would only lie to him in his all too obvious weakness. He told himself to remain calm, but remaining calm was not easy, especially in the face of Elizabeth's mad trombonist, whom he kept imagining over and over again until he became so real that he could swear to hearing snatches of his music. Sometimes he could not believe that Maureen could be so shamelessly unfaithful and he would wonder if Elizabeth had actually witnessed the trombonist or if in her obsession with Snoddy she had imagined him. But on other days he would see his sister as a coarse-minded slut, driven by lust and a low peasant cunning that tried to conceal it.

Elizabeth came in the evenings, cooked him a meal, and sat at the bedside recounting the advantages of Larch Lawn over Clonglass.

"We could be very happy there," she said. "All that's needed is the will to move. Because you were born here, because it's your father's house, you think you are tied to it, but think of the unnecessary expense of spirit in a life with Maureen and Snoddy. I'm much better since I moved, and I'd feel even better if you were with me."

"We'll see" was his evasive reply. "I'll wait till I've recovered first. A man should never make an important decision while he's under the weather."

He got up the following week, but he remained near the house, not wishing to tempt providence again by premature exposure to heat and cold. The days were uncommonly warm for mid-September, and he strolled in the yard watching the restless Henry, or in Rowan's Field watching Snoddy draw in bales of barley straw for bedding and fodder. He felt as if he'd been away for a long time. Everything looked slightly unfamiliar, as if he were seeing it in a dream, and when he got up on the tractor and started the engine he took childish pleasure in selecting the gears. He was pleased with this year's winter barley. He would sow again in October, and he would sow more this time, because income from winter fattening was unlikely to improve. Thinking about something other than Maureen and Snoddy had cleared his head. From his tractor seat the world looked a much saner place than from the sickroom window.

While still too weak to work, he went for walks in the fields and laid plans for the coming winter and spring. After he had been on his feet for a week, he went for a longer walk. It was a calm day with a bluish haze over Slieve Bloom and the smell of burning stubble from a nearby field. He watched a neighbour hauling a burning tire over the barley stubble and made his way along the tree-lined lane that led to the Grove, pleased that his legs no longer trembled and that he no longer needed his overcoat to keep warm in the sun. The warmth of the sun on his neck and his awareness of returning strength gave him a sense of physical well-being that only increased as he squatted at stool in a clump of ferns in the shade of a slender larch. He was fond of squatting in brakes. He firmly believed that the best reason for living in the country was the ease with which a busy man could respond to nature's call in the open air, a pleasure that far excelled huntin', shootin', fishin', and tumblin' in haystacks. He was particularly fond of responding to the call in the Grove, if only because the aspiring larches and the nervous melodies of the birds took his mind off the incongruity of evacuation and filled him with intimations of airy eternities.

Pup usually accompanied him on these expeditions, and more often than not joined him in the payment of nature's tribute. Pup took the manner of payment seriously. He would quarter a clearing before choosing a clean patch of ground, then arch his back and, in pressing, grimace as painfully as if he were passing razor blades. Kevin, at least on this occasion, paid his tribute less histrionically, but he could not help thinking that in coming to the Grove he had behaved more like a dog than a horse or bull. A horse will eliminate, as Festus would say, at full gallop and a bull will do the same without pausing in his grazing; but man and his best friend concentrate on defecation to the exclusion of all other activity, though Festus had told him that he once knew an Englishman who played the tuba on the commode. Perhaps this was why the Anglo-Saxons were superior to the Celts in science and technology. Quite simply, they had mastered the means of doing two impossible things at the same time.

He was so enchanted by the felicity of his thought that an alien smell had enveloped him before he became aware that it was not his own. He looked to right and left and over his shoulder, and he saw Pup's dead body hanging from a drooping branch of the Pooka Tree. Having wiped himself with a handful of fern leaves, he hitched up his trousers and walked uncomprehendingly round the object that was once his dog.

"Who could have killed a harmless pup?" he asked aloud.

"Snoddy," he said. "It was no one but Snoddy."

"Where is Pup?" he asked the Ruminant when he got back to the house.

"That's something I had meant to tell you. He vanished a fortnight ago and I haven't seen him since."

"Come with me. I've got something to show you."

They walked down the lane and along the road to the Grove while Snoddy talked of the moisture content of this year's barley and Kevin listened in silence as if the barley wasn't his.

"That's Pup," Kevin said when they reached the Pooka Tree.

"That was Pup."

"He was a stupid dog, but he did nothing that deserved hanging. Did you do it for a cod or for revenge?"

"What do you mean?"

"It was you that did it, wasn't it?"

"If you want to know, it was Her Ladyship, she of Larch Lawn. Pup was always trying to sniff her knickers, and she couldn't understand it, simple woman."

Kevin lashed out with his fist and caught Snoddy on the tip of the chin. Snoddy reeled, tried to recover his balance, and fell backwards over a log with both his legs in the air.

"If you want to live to draw your pension, you won't mention Elizabeth like that again."

Snoddy got slowly to his feet and shook himself like a dog that had come out of a river. Then he bent his head and rushed at Kevin like a butting goat. Kevin sidestepped and tried to trip him, but Snoddy gripped him round the waist and brought him down with a dunt. Kevin tried to turn, but in a flash Snoddy was standing over him, twisting his left arm and crushing his windpipe with his boot.

"I've taken your measure and it's short," Snoddy said. "I was wondering when you'd lose your temper, and now you've lost it. At first I thought it would be over Maureen, and then over Elizabeth, but life was more ingenious—you lost it over a dog. We can live in peace, you and me, provided you live and let love. You can have Her Ladyship and I'll have your sister, and I promise to say nothing of what went before. But I think Maureen would be happier if you followed your wife to Larch Lawn."

When Snoddy had gone, he picked himself up, sore with humiliation. He was still weak, and Snoddy had taken advantage of his weakness, but he would never give him such an opportunity again.

Dinner was on the table when he got back, and Snoddy was sitting in his place.

"That's my place you're sitting in," he said.

Snoddy got up and went to the other end of the table. "I'm a reasonable man. I sat in your place and did your duty while you were in bed, but now I'm willing to play second fiddle again. It's the way of the world, a day up and a day down." He winked at Maureen.

As she dished out the steaming parsnip cubes, she bubbled with good humour. She joked with Snoddy about Kevin's mustard, and Kevin could see that she knew about his humiliation in the Grove. During his illness they had become accustomed to referring to him ironically as the Man Upstairs, and now they talked about him in his presence as if he were still upstairs. Looking at Maureen, he realized that if he were to be master in his own house he would have to reassert himself forcefully and soon.

After they had eaten he said that he was going to lie down and took his mug of tea upstairs. He did not go to bed, however. He sat on the table by the window, sipping his tea and looking down on two old hens feathering themselves under a tree. After five minutes Maureen crossed the yard with an empty basin, and Snoddy followed her round behind the hay shed.

He took another five minutes over his tea, then went downstairs and out into the yard. This year's bales were stacked high in the hay shed and a red metal ladder stood against them. Carefully, he climbed up to the top and looked across the flat bed of bales under the corrugated iron roof. It was the obvious place, the most comfortable place, but they weren't there. Next he went into the old stable and looked into the empty mangers, then into the cow house, but it seemed that they had vanished into thin air. He opened the door of the old dairy, where he now kept the oats crusher and the freezer, but all he disturbed was a rat that jumped into a corner behind some hundredweight bags of pollard. Weak at the knees, he sat down on one of the bags and wondered if they had gone out into the fields, but there were so many fields and so many hiding places under hedges.

Beside the freezer was a pair of Elizabeth's pink Wellingtons, and as he looked at the pointed toes, he was shocked at the sense of loathing that burst inside him. Loathing for what? he asked himself and waited in vain for an answer. He had often seen his wife in pink Wellingtons without looking twice at them, but now, as they stood before him, his loathing gave way to a sense of constriction. Without her, he would be a freer man, but would he be a happier man? Since his marriage he felt as if he had a firmer stake in the land, and at times he even felt at peace with himself. But the price was high. A man, it seemed, was not complete without a woman, but in giving him a sense of completion she surrounded him with a moat of ifs and buts. In spite of all, he was strong enough to go his own way, but as he went his way he was aware of a sense of abrasion.

Like all men, he was subject to irrational impulses, but never more so than since he married her. Was what Festus said true, that women were less rational than men, the vectors of the dread disease of unreason? If only he could wash from himself the taint of the irrational, leach away his petty preoccupations with people and events, with Elizabeth, Maureen, and Snoddy. They were the grist that the quernstones of the mind ground and ground until they ended by grinding their own edges. The only escape was to think of open fields of barley shaking in the wind, a world of sanity, of evident cause and effect, compared with the steaming ragout that was life in the kitchen. He thought of his old relationship with Maureen, gentle and comforting and seemingly endless, like summer drizzle slanting over unclipped hedges. They had lived together in unconsidered ease and now that life was lost, never again to be recovered. Perhaps Festus was right after all. A bad woman was bad, but a good woman was worse.

As he raised his head, a beam of sunlight from the open door caught a pinch of fine dust drifting down from between the timbers of the ceiling. He stored the oats in the loft above the crusher, and the only access to it was up some stone steps built outside against the gable. He went into the stable and took down the horsewhip that hung coiled above the door. Outside, he cracked it a few times as if testing a stiff wrist, and Henry, hearing the snap, bellowed and came out of his loose box. He tiptoed up the steps and opened the door of the oats loft. The two of them were only half clothed, lying on a bed of uncrushed oats, Snoddy driving downwards and Maureen's hips rising against him. Snoddy looked up, but before he could wink, the whip had cut across his narrow backside. As he swore hell-fire, Kevin brought down the whip again beside the first red line. He raised it a third time, but Snoddy rolled over on his back with Maureen on top for protection.

Staring at her dimpled buttocks, Kevin coiled the whip, closed the door, and bolted it from the outside.

"You'll pay for this, you madman," Snoddy called after him, but he went down the steps without replying.

He went into the kitchen, took down his shotgun from above the dresser, and put two cartridges in the breech. He climbed the steps again, opened the door, and motioned them both to come out. Snoddy had pulled up his trousers and Maureen had pulled down her skirt, and there was a hollow in the heap of oats where they had lain.

"You'll rue this," said Snoddy, feeling his backside with his fingertips.

"I'm going to give you one minute to clear off this farm. If you don't hop to it now, I'll pepper your whipped arse with the best buckshot."

"You'll have less to say when Her Ladyship hears about your dirty tricks."

"Scram," he said, bringing up the gun barrels and cocking the safety catch.

He poked him in the back with the muzzle and marched him down the lane. Seeing one of his neighbours leaning over a gate, he raised the gun and fired one barrel in the air. Snoddy gave a jump and began running with his hands over his head.

"If you ever show your frog's face on my farm again, I'll tear you apart limb from limb," he called after him.

"What was all that about?" the neighbour asked him.

"He's been hanging round Maureen ever since he came here. Didn't give her a minute's peace, the mangy bugger. And when I warned him off, he had the gall to say that I fancied her for myself—my own sister!"

"The world is full of badness," said his neighbour. "And the good are not much better than the bad."

Kevin was pleased that the farmer had seen him. He would tell the story in the pub that evening, and by tomorrow everyone in the area would know that Snoddy had been lusting after Maureen and had become so insane in his lust that he accused her brother of lusting after her as well. Even if Snoddy tried to spread stories about incest in the afternoon, nobody would now believe him. All in all, things could not have worked out better.

Maureen was sobbing in the kitchen when he got back.

"You had to do it. You couldn't fast for a week or two while I was sick, could you?"

"He made me do it," she cried. "He threatened to tell Elizabeth about us two if I didn't."

"I thought that was just what you wanted."

"I'm not that bad," she moaned. "It was just that he gave me no peace."

"You'll have all the peace in the world now," he said, putting the gun back in its place above the dresser.

That evening he drove down to Larch Lawn to tell Elizabeth the good news.

"Snoddy is gone. I put a gun in his back and chased him down the lane. You can come home now."

"Did you see Maureen off as well?"

"What has she got to do with it?"

"It's either one of us or the other. Quite simply, you can't have both."

"I can't show my own sister the door."

"Leave her at Clonglass and come down here to me. It isn't too far to come, is it?"

"I'll think about it," he said, knowing that she had defeated him.

12

November 1st
From the kitchen window I watched him coming through
the Wide Gate with the calves. In everything he does is the
inevitability of authenticity. He may be aware of other ways
of doing things, but from the way he chooses flows the
grace that slays the demon self-consciousness. If only I could
put on his intuitive knowledge like a coat and exude with
him the aroma of hedge and field. I took his old tweed
jacket from the peg in the hallway and sat at the piano. The
lining was torn and it hung loosely from my too-narrow
shoulders, one pocket heavy with clamps and bolts. I played
Liszt's "Liebestraum" in A flat major and Grieg's "Wedding
Day at Troldhaugen," and he came through the door with a
peal of incredulous laughter.

"You'd make a fine scarecrow," he said, but when I
grasped his hand he did not kiss me as I had expected.

She closed her diary and went to the parlour window.

The day was mild, with a clear sky and a sharp lukewarm sun. It had been a mild autumn so far, and the leaves, though changed to yellow and lighter greens, still clung to the branches of the trees. Kevin had sown the winter barley, and now he was in the field by the Grove ploughing for winter wheat. As she thought of him, she imagined him perched on the new tractor that Murt bought, moving slowly and precisely up and down, looking back over his right shoulder at the cleanly turning sod. Since he had joined her at Larch Lawn in the beginning of October she had never known such domestic peace. At last they had privacy, a house to themselves where they could sit in the evenings listening to the ticking of the clock. For a man of his character he had an unerring sense of delicacy. Since she had grown big, he never forced himself upon her in bed, and now he seldom went out in the evenings. He had stopped going to Phelan's on Saturdays. He was in all respects a happily married man. If he had a fault, it was not a fault of character. It was merely his lack of music. Sometimes she would ask him to come into the parlour, but she knew that Chopin made him yawn, that only Irish ballads could enliven his flagging interest.

The mildness of the morning enticed her into the open air. She got into her car and drove down the road to the Grove. Before her was a big Ford travelling along the straight road, two farmers in the front with their caps sitting at different angles, the driver's over his right ear, the passenger's over his left. They were travelling at speed, hurrying to the mart and then to the pub, looking straight ahead, unaware of the day in their headlong conversation. Seeing them, these typical midland men, gave her an inexplicable sense of comfort, of all being right with the world, of being part of that world, the world of practical men, the world of work rather than thought, and she felt that it would be nice to follow them into Killage, stand beside them in the mart, and join in a snatch of their conversation.

A drove of bullocks spilled out of a hidden laneway, followed by an old man with an ashplant. She pulled up, opened the window, and watched him dragging his down-turned Wellingtons so that the heels made a slithering sound on the road with each step. He was wearing a bandless felt hat with a battered brim sloping down over his ears, and his narrow eyes stared unseeingly into the distance while the dimple in his prominent chin, like the misplaced eye of a Cyclops, focused unavailingly on the rumps of his cattle. She waited for him to say "Day," and when he didn't she said it herself, and he raised his ashplant in a flamboyantly generous salute.

She parked the car and walked slowly towards the Grove as the white scut of a rabbit vanished into a ditch. Bars of sunlight slanted between trees, catching the occasional leaf fluttering down the autumn-scented air. She sat on a log under an oak while the falling acorns pattered among the ferns, and she decided to make a batch of scones in the afternoon for Kevin's evening tea. Surrounded by minute sounds that fell singly into bottomless silence, she felt herself move with the swing of the earth, but when she looked at her feet she was sitting in the same place. It was something that the Grove always did to her, filled her with a sense of the numinous, made her wish for incomparable talent and intelligence and the company of young poets, though her common sense told her that they were likely to be selfish, self-centred, and too impoverished to afford the best dry sherry.

"Please, God," she said aloud, "give me grace to accept my lot, to love Kevin for the good and simple man that he is, to reject impure thoughts about fair-haired musicians with fine hair on their delicate wrists, and grant me the virtue of humility and resignation. Burn out of my heart, O Lord, the vice of hypercriticism, that thrusting outrider of rampant egotism."

The sound of her words made her stiffen as she realized that the person who said them could not conceivably be part of the world of the two farmers in the Ford. She felt that already she had moved too far from Kevin, that they would both need to start again at the age of eight, shipwrecked together on an island like a boy and girl in a story she had read as a child:

"Where did you get it?" he asked when she came back to the hut with a baby son in her arms.
"I found it in the wood," she said.
"It's a baby," he told her.
"I know," she replied.

She wanted to be like that boy and girl, to burn her books and sheet music, to learn from Kevin the song of sensuous experience and from her son the purpose of her breasts.

But she was being foolish, she told herself. She and Kevin had already sunk comfortably into the rut of good habits on which all happy marriages were founded. She had proof of that last night when she woke up to find him rummaging in her knickers. She listened to his deep, even breathing and realized that he was asleep, that only his hands were awake. An image of perfection in the marriage of man and woman came to her, a saying from Isaiah that she remembered from the convent: "The wolf also shall dwell with the lamb, and the leopard shall lie down with the kid."

Pursued by the song of an ebullient thrush, she walked back down the lane and waited as she saw the postman dismount from his bicycle on the slight incline.

"Have you anything for me today?" she asked.

"A brown letter for Kevin and a white one for you."

As soon as he had gone, she opened the envelope and read the brief but lucid note:

Dear Mrs. Hurley,
In innocence you married an unnatural man. It is common knowl-
edge that your husband lies with his sister, but can a just God
punish you for something you didn't know? More of that soon from
A Distant but Genuine Admirer

She folded the letter and started the car, telling herself that unless she hurried home the roast would be overdone. As she drove, a phrase from the letter kept flashing at the back of her mind, as if someone was shuffling a pack of cards inside her head. It had come from "a distant admirer" but not an admirer of Kevin. It more than likely came from Billy Snoddy, but why had he waited a month before sending it? Did he wish her to be more advanced in pregnancy, thinking perhaps that she would be more vulnerable to evil suggestion at five months than four? Clearly, his intentions were not good. He wished her to fall victim to vague suspicions that she could not verify. She could not ask Kevin if he lay with his sister, and neither could she ask anyone else. But the story was patently ridiculous. While she lived at Clonglass, she had never been aware of any attachment between Kevin and Maureen. The attachment, if such existed, was between Maureen and Snoddy. She would not show the letter to Kevin. It would only make him angry and, if he broke Snoddy's neck "in at least two places" as he often threatened, get him into trouble with the police.

She took the rib of beef out of the oven and poured the water off the carrots and peas into a jug for gravy. She had cooked both the carrots and peas with the joint in the oven because it was less trouble, and she had baked five large potatoes in tinfoil, four for Kevin and one for herself. Gradually, she was getting him accustomed to the idea of eating less potato and more parsnips, peas, swedes, and carrots, of which they had plenty on the farm. She had also tried to wean him off mustard, reminding him that good cooking was wasted on a man who smothered everything in condiments, but he only said that he knew what he liked, and that he liked mustard. The business of laying the table and getting up the dinner made her forget the letter, and it was only when she saw him coming across the yard with his jacket on one shoulder that she wondered again if she should tell him.

They fell to the minestrone soup without speaking, but she drew comfort from the fact that he was eating it at all and from the homely slurping sounds he made with his spoon. Soup before beef was a revolution in his life, believing as he did in "dry packing." When she first suggested that they should have soup from Hallowe'en till May Day and none for the rest of the year, he asked for an explanation; and when she told him that the ancient Fianna lived indoors from November to May and in the open for the rest of the year, he laughed and said that it was the only good reason for eating soup he'd ever heard. She expected him to pass comment, but he pushed his plate aside and waited with obvious impatience for the real dinner.

"It's the first day of the Soup Year," she said when she saw that he was determined to keep his opinion to himself.

"So I see."

"I thought you'd notice." She smiled.

"I think you're giving me soup so that I'll eat less. It fills a man up before he starts."

"Did you like it?"

"I prefer dry fodder. I might have it after my meat in future."

"No, you won't. You'll have it before the main course like any Christian."

She took the plates from the oven and they ate in silence, but she knew that he would speak as soon as he had taken the edge off his appetite.

"I'm going to get the north pasture tested for lime before the weather breaks," he said, halving a potato as if his knife were an executioner's sword.

"It mightn't break for another month. After the late spring it's a lovely autumn."

"It was a late year. If you went by the weather and not the calendar, as any good farmer must, you wouldn't start soup for another month."

Again they were silent, aware of the ticking of the clock.

"Are you going to do anything about the ragwort in Jack's?" she asked.

"I'll spray it as soon as the cattle come off it."

"Noonan said yesterday that we should run one or two ewes with the dry cattle to keep it under control."

"I don't like sheep," he said, as if there was no more to say.

He was attacking his heaped-up plate with gusto, putting plenty of butter on the baked potatoes and plenty of mustard on the beef. Sitting at the head of the table, he seemed to occupy its whole breadth. His shoulders were heavy and broad, and the sleeves of his check shirt were rolled up to the elbow, so that when he raised his fork the thicket of dark hair on his arm seemed to ripple like grass in a stiff breeze. His open-collared shirt revealed a sturdy neck with sinews like bull wire under the berry-brown skin, and his black wavy hair was closely cropped above the ears and combed back from a forehead that was too high for the rest of his face. He looked the picture of vigour and physical well-being, and she felt herself flush with the sudden warmth of her feeling for him.

"It's well for men," she said. "Women are frail as gewgaws by comparison."

"There are women who wouldn't say that."

"Men are stronger. They keep their good looks longer—"

"And they die sooner," he said dryly.

"A man of fifty can look as handsome as a man of thirty, but at fifty most women, especially mothers, are shapeless dumplings."

"You'll never be a dumpling, Elizabeth."

"I'll be glad when this is over. I'm not sure I want to go through it again."

"We'll see."

"I'm very fertile, though you wouldn't think it to look at me. I fell in the first week."

"Will you get me my beer?" he said. "The soup has made me thirsty."

Knowing that women's talk embarrassed him, she rose to get his ale though she herself had not finished. While she was on her feet, she filled the kettle and put it on the gas.

"Don't make tea for me," he said.

"Surely you'll have a cup and a piece of the fresh cake."

"I'm going up to Clonglass to look at a heifer. I'll have a drop there before I come back."

Without knowing why, she was distressed to hear that he was going to Clonglass without his tea. She realized that he went to Clonglass every day, that he had to because of the farm, but she would have preferred him to go in the mornings, not immediately after dinner. Somehow she had always imagined him in the fields, not in the house, but if he had his tea there he was bound to see Maureen, who was her enemy. She could not bear to think of him talking to her, laughing at her coarse humour, perhaps laughing at a joke about "the quare one."

The following week she received another anonymous letter, longer, more mysterious, more disturbing:

Dear Mrs. Hurley,
Kevin's search for a wife began with his sister, but his incest didn't end with his marriage. It still goes on. All afternoon farming at Clonglass ends in the double bed, but the punishment, you may have noticed, falls elsewhere. The pattern is already set. First Murt, then the boy Breffny, then your dog Judy. Who is next? You or your child? The punishment of the evildoers will come, not here, but hereafter, while those who are close to them in this life must die. Flee the Wrath to Come today.

So says a Distant but Devoted
Well-Wisher

Though she did not for a moment believe that Kevin went to bed with his sister, the letter disturbed her more than the first. She could not help asking herself if he was somehow jinxed, the innocent victim of the wrath of a capricious God. His best friend had died, then his nephew, and finally her lovely Labrador, and what had he done to deserve it? It was not a subject she could discuss with him. Even if he himself were conscious of indiscriminate vengeance, he would laugh to reassure her and rightly tell her that her fears rose from superstition, not religion.

As the December days shortened and the dark evenings drew in, she grew slower and heavier and more self-absorbed. She was in the seventh month of pregnancy, and she required all her strength to cook Kevin's meals and keep the house tidy. Pregnancy was a most unnatural condition, she thought. There were women who were born for motherhood, big, broody dams with wide hips and heavy eyes and breasts, who were not themselves unless they were breeding, but she was not one of them. Pregnancy was like being invaded by an alien intelligence that sought to change the temper of your mind and body, that unsettled you with the most ludicrous fads. She could no longer stand the smell of coffee or sherry, nor the smell of Kevin's pipe, but she could not get enough marshmallows, though she had never been conscious of liking them before. So far the worst time was when morning sickness began in the third month. She would wake up with a sense of nausea, and after retching unsuccessfully over the washbasin she would go downstairs for a cup of tea only to run immediately to vomit in the kitchen sink.

She went to Dr. Blizzard, who weighed her as if she were a bullock in a cattle mart and gave her what he euphemistically termed "an internal." He put her lying on his narrow couch and made her open her legs wide so that he could rummage inside her with God knows what. A gloved hand? A fire tongs? A wooden ladle? The stem of a Peterson pipe? She felt half a dozen incongruous objects prodding her in quick succession, and she thought that she would sob in her lonely helplessness. She had always regarded her vagina as her very own. She could never understand women who did not share her strong proprietorial instinct, women whose vaginas were concourses through which whole generations of young men passed without meeting or passing the time of night. She felt so strongly about the privacy of her body that it was only by an effort of will that she could acknowledge the rights that Kevin had acquired in marriage. But here was a blasé old man poking about inside her as if she were a grate in an old-fashioned fireplace. Beyond doubt or exaggeration, it was the most distasteful thing that had ever happened to her. After one visit to Blizzard, after hearing him breathe the word "hyperemesis" as if he had invented it, she prayed that she would never become pregnant again. She also prayed for a boy, because she knew that if it were a girl, Kevin's paternal instinct would merely be aroused, not satisfied. She composed a little ejaculation which she said morning and evening and at odd moments during the day:

> Give me grace, O Lord, to withstand the perils of
> pregnancy and all its indignities.
> O Lord, hear my prayer and, if it be your will,
> may I never fall again.

Though the saying of the prayer gave her comfort as she crept up the stairs on hands and knees or leant against a wall until the cramps left her legs, she could not help wondering if it was the kind of aspiration the Good and Bounteous Lord wished to hear from a member of the Irish Countrywomen's Association.

Pregnancy was not her only worry. Her psoriasis, which in the September sun seemed to be receding, had become uglier, angrier, more obnoxious. She could not bear to look at her hands, because when she did, she asked herself if her child would inherit her condition. Her thoughts became so obsessive that the burden of them was almost unbearable. The dark miasma that had surrounded Clonglass had come to envelop the once-airy Larch Lawn, and she was powerless to escape its influence, and Kevin was powerless to protect her against something that only existed in her thoughts.

One night while he was reading, she became so restless that she went out to the gable of the house for air. A full moon with a big sad face was sitting on the hedge by the gate. The slight haze in the east had given it a softly yellow hue, and above it was a wavy wisp of cloud like an eyebrow over an eye. She stood looking at it for a long time, seeing it finally as an all-knowing Oriental face impassive in the midst of adversity. It was such an unusual moon that she could not help thinking of it as a heavenly sign that she had come to the end of her suffering. She returned to the house and sat at the end of the table writing her diary:

I am heavy like a cow in calf. I can't even play the piano. I lie on the settee and roll off it on all fours like a whale with arms and legs. Kevin makes fun of me and I laugh, but I know that this is not a joke. On good days I pray that my child will be handsome and intelligent and, more, that he will develop as a man. I never developed as a woman. At twenty I was as I am now—more or less. In Dublin an enthusiastic student tried to convert me to Marxism, but I laughed at the absurdity of his great exemplar. His favourite quotation—"The workers have nothing to lose but their chains"—seemed so puerile, so simplistic, so untrue that I was convinced that a woman who could see through such vulgar trumpery at twenty must have great things in store for her. But today I am merely that young woman. On bad days I am unable to pray. How, I ask myself, can I pray to a God who may be plotting my destruction? Then I shudder at the thought that I may never suckle my child, that this unnatural charade will have been for nothing. Tonight, however, it suddenly came to me that I have come through. I saw a moon that was obviously meant for me, a sad but wise moon with a face that had known jaundice and sorrow but goodness too. I know that I have come to the end of a long night, that tomorrow I shall find strength to burn the next letter without reading it, that God is good, not indifferent or bad.

She closed her diary and went out again to the gable. The yellow haze had lifted. The moon was plain-faced and bright, the wavy eyebrow gone.

December was dark and wet. Light came just before nine and failed again at half-past two. Clouds, low and grey, rolled over empty fields into the east to be followed by even greyer clouds from the west. Now and again a watery pool of light in the grey would hint at a far-off sun, slipping elusively over the horizon on its short journey from southeast to southwest. In the garden the dark trees dripped endlessly on poached turf, showering her with droplets whenever she went to the clothesline; and in the house, in spite of the central heating, sudden draughts made her shiver in such a way that she thought the baby in her womb shivered too.

Her baby was now a living presence, kicking and elbowing, filling her with weird spasms of excitement. But in spite of the Oriental moon, she had not altogether conquered her anxieties. She managed to burn the letters without reading them, telling herself in the day that irrational fear, not God, was her greatest enemy; but in the night she would wake up hot and trembling after shouting for human comfort in the nightmare of a fire-licked forest.

On the Saturday before Christmas she drove up the mountain to Patsy Darcy's for her Christmas turkey. She was delighted to get away from the house, to relax behind the wheel of the Mercedes, driving northwards into moorland under a washed-out sky. She would have found it difficult to squeeze into her Mini, but the Mercedes was roomy and comfortable, purring quietly but powerfully on little hills and taking off like a greyhound from blind crossroads. Sometimes, for fun, she would imitate Kevin, leaning over the wheel with her left hand on her knee, and she would wonder how it felt to drive with a trailer in tow and if peace of mind would perhaps return in February with the birth of her child.

Patsy Darcy was in the yard mixing boiled potatoes with crushed oats in a wooden tub. Tall, white-haired, and mad as a March hare, he straightened his back and peered at her with one frail hand over his eyes. He had spent his middle years in an asylum without uttering a word until one day he made a joke of such ingenious obscenity that the doctor, in a fit of unaccustomed and unprofessional good humour, discharged him on the spot. Now he lived alone on his ruined farm with six dry cattle, a sheepdog, and a flock of turkeys which he fattened for the Christmas trade. His grandmother was killed in 1920 by drunken Black and Tans who ran her down in their Crossley and dumped her broken body on a roadside dunghill. Though Patsy did not remember her, he never forgot her death, not even in the years of silence in the asylum. Now, as a gesture of reparation, or perhaps as a means of setting to rights what he saw as the unfinished business of history, he gave each of his turkeys, irrespective of its sex, a typically English male Christian name—Herbert, Harold, Kenneth, Alec, or Graham—and in preparation for the knife and the table fed them all they could eat in an old cow house warmed by a storage heater that ran on peat briquettes. In spite of the questionable view of history to which they owed their full crops, his turkeys were highly prized. Everyone who considered himself anyone ate "a turkey of Patsy Darcy's" for Christmas.

"You want a turkey, hee," he shouted and ran towards the house with his bottom sticking out behind.

She stood uncertainly in the yard, inhaling the sour smell of mash from the tub until he returned with a lantern, which he held before him shoulder high.

"You want a turkey, hee." He hopped with glee to her side.

She followed him into the dark cow house, where two splay-footed birds, heavy as pregnant women, were pecking in the glow of the heater.

"I've only got two left and one of them is bespoke."

"One will do."

"This is George. He's twenty-two pounds," he said after reading the label on the bird's neck.

"A smaller bird would have done, but I'll take him."

"He's not as heavy as David, but David, surname Lloyd George, is not for sale. I've earmarked him for myself."

"Lloyd George wasn't English," she told him.

"No, but in his time he ate many an English turkey."

He was standing over her with shaggy shoulder-length hair, the lantern lifted to her face so that she could get the smell of stale sweat from his oxter.

"As a little favour, I ask all my customers to refer to their bird by its Christian name, especially at table on Christmas Day. You will say, for example, 'Another slice of George, my dear?' or 'George's neck and giblets will make fine soup tomorrow.' It's a small enough favour. Otherwise I don't sell. Do you promise to call him George, hee?"

He had moved closer to her, fixing her with mad, staring eyes. She felt his gaze like a cold wind on her body, prematurely exposing her child to the icy rudeness of the world. The walls seemed to move towards her under the light of the lantern. She felt her legs shake, and the next thing she knew she was hurrying towards the car.

"Come back," he called. "He's a lovely bird, every bit as good as David, surname Lloyd George."

She drove furiously down the lane, watching his wild waving in the rearview mirror, glad to have escaped from she knew not what enormity. It was not Patsy Darcy she feared most, however. It was the mad subterranean current in her life, and she prayed aloud as she hugged the wheel: "Protect me from the dark, O Lord, and give me the sanity of cleansing light."

She bought a frozen turkey in the supermarket in Killage, because now she could not bear the thought of plucking a fresh one. Carrying it to the car in a plastic bag seemed such a sane, uncomplicated thing that she could have cried with relief. And when someone spoke to her in the street, she smiled with pleasure because it proved that she was herself after all, recognizable to others as an ordinary, simple human being.

The following day Kevin said that they could not allow Maureen to eat her Christmas dinner alone.

"But if we invite her, we'll have her for the whole day and maybe the whole night too," Elizabeth said.

"No, we won't. I'll drive her home as soon as dinner is over."

"But she'll degrade everything with coarse talk. I had intended opening a bottle of wine—"

"What has that got to do with Maureen?"

"Oh, invite her if you must."

"I'll tell her to behave. She's my own sister. I can't leave her to spend the first Christmas since my father's death in a lonely house alone."

"If you invite her, you'll have to look after her."

"If nothing else, she'll wash up after dinner and you can put up your feet."

"That's all I need, Maureen splashing about in my kitchen."

Christmas Day was dry with an icy wind flinging dust and twigs against the windowpanes. They braved the cold to go to early Mass, and at one Kevin drove to Clongiass to fetch Maureen while Elizabeth made the bread sauce. Maureen arrived in a grey overcoat and a woollen scarf swaddled three times round her neck. Elizabeth had misjudged the turkey. She had expected it to be done at two, but when she tested it, she decided that it would take another half-hour.

While they waited, Kevin poured himself a pint of ale and sat down to talk to Maureen.

"Are you going to offer me a drink?" she asked him.

"I didn't know you wanted one. Is it a glass of ale that's on your mind?"

"No, it's a glass of whiskey. The cold got into me cy-

218

cling to Mass this morning, and it's still in the marrow of my bones."

He gave her a glass of whiskey with plenty of water, and when she had drunk it she asked for another. Elizabeth frowned as he poured it, but Maureen was eager for warmth and her brother was not averse to pleasing her.

While they talked about their dead father, Elizabeth busied herself between the cooker and the table, aware of her awkwardness but glad that at last the turkey was done.

"He lived long enough," Kevin said.

"That's what I thought the day he died," Maureen replied. "But now I'm not so sure. He took with him what warmth was left in the house. It was a cold stand at the best of times, but Mammy's death made it colder and Daddy's froze it altogether."

After Kevin had carved, they all sat round the table with the light on because it was already dark outside. Kevin poured himself another pint of ale, saying that he was dispensing with dry packing for one day in the year, and Elizabeth reluctantly shared her bottle of claret with Maureen.

"Do you remember what Old Lar Gorman used to say to us on the way home from school?" Maureen asked Kevin, and when he said that he'd forgotten she choked with laughter and spilt her wine over the linen tablecloth.

Elizabeth pretended not to see or hear. She was determined to ignore Maureen for an hour, but she could not help telling herself that the meal she had slaved so hard to prepare had been reduced by contamination to pig's swill.

"Do you remember what we used to do in the Grove on the way to the moor with the cows?" Maureen asked Kevin.

The whiskey and wine had taken their toll. She was poised over her plate like a clumsy clucking hen, and every now and then she would laugh trumpetingly and put out her tongue before lifting another awkward forkful. There was nothing for Elizabeth to say, because the subject of conversation was a mystery to her. It was as if Maureen realized that her sister-in-law had spent her formative years in a convent and was determined to talk only of things that happened while she was away. Elizabeth told herself to hear no evil, but when Maureen began tugging at Kevin's sleeve she had to offer up a little aspiration to maintain her equanimity.

"God forgive me, I nearly laughed out loud at Mass this morning when I saw Billy Snoddy going to the rails for Communion. I never see him but I think of the Lad in the Corner, and I never think of the Lad in the Corner but I go into kinks laughing. Do you ever think of the Lad in the Corner, Kevin?"

"I have more to think about than that."

"He changed Snoddy's life and he changed mine. And when you think about it, he changed yours and maybe Elizabeth's too."

"Who, may I ask, is the influential Lad in the Corner?" Elizabeth turned to Kevin.

"Will I tell her, Kevin?"

"Can't you think of something better to talk about on Christmas Day?"

"The Lad in the Corner is not for ladies." Maureen giggled.

Kevin looked warily at Elizabeth as his sister spluttered with suppressed merriment and upset an empty wineglass with her arm.

"If a real lady saw the Lad in the Corner, she'd die of shock," Maureen said. "Some ladies are so refined that they would faint at the smell of him."

"Who is the Lad in the Corner, Kevin?" Elizabeth demanded. "I must and shall know."

"It's no subject for the dinner table," Kevin said uncomfortably.

"How dare you!" Elizabeth shouted. "How dare you come here on Christmas Day and scandalize my husband and me with disgusting innuendo!"

For a moment a tense hush hung over the table while the wind snarled in the chimney. Then Maureen hooted contemptuously, drank the last of the wine from Elizabeth's glass, and said very quietly, "He was my husband before he was yours."

"And what does that mean?" Elizabeth demanded coolly.

"Only this. He lay with me *before* he lay with you. And if it pleases Your Ladyship, he lay with me *after* as well."

Elizabeth felt the strength ebb from her arms and legs. The fork fell from her fingers and she swallowed against a rising tide of nausea.

"How dare you say such a thing on Our Lord's birthday," she managed to get out.

"Come on, Kevin"—Maureen laughed—"tell her why you turn to me. Tell her why she's no good in bed."

Elizabeth looked at Kevin, but he emptied his glass and stared at a clean plate.

"How can you sit through all that and say nothing?" she asked him.

"You have no idea of the secret acts that tether a man to a woman's apron strings. If you come to bed with me, I'll show you," Maureen said.

Elizabeth had no idea how she got up the stairs. She was lying on the bed sobbing wildly, a great weight on her belly crushing both herself and her child, her skull contracted into a hard knot of pain. She was all alone, far from the comfort of human voices, scrabbling in the dark, now on her feet, now on her hands and knees, exposed to searing winds, but before her was a black forest where no breath of air disturbed the thick undergrowth between the trees. It was a place of warmth and secrecy, and there she was going for shelter and forgetfulness, away from the rough edge of the world.

13

"Why did you have to go and say that?" Kevin asked.

"She brought it on herself with all her fine airs. I'm not good enough for her and neither are you."

"It was a senseless thing to do."

He drove her home in silence and cleared away the dinner things when he got back. He felt at once benumbed and afraid of the outline of something he could not quite discern in his mind. After a while he went upstairs to find her asleep over the bedclothes, and he got a blanket from the linen press and spread it over her shoulders.

He went up again before bedtime and said to her, "Elizabeth, you mustn't worry. It isn't good for yourself or the child."

He felt such a rush of tenderness for her that he wanted to hold her in his arms all night as she slept, but he felt too formless, too remote from what he normally regarded as himself, to make a move in her direction.

"Please go away . . . and switch off the light," she said without opening her eyes.

He went to the linen press again for blankets and sheets and made a bed for himself in the next room. For a long time he lay in the dark, unable to think or sleep, and then suddenly he heard a cry.

"Was that you, Elizabeth?" he asked at her door.

"Get the doctor quick" was all she said.

He telephoned Dr. Blizzard, cursing with impatience as the phone rang and rang.

"What's the matter with her?" the doctor asked.

"She isn't feeling well."

"Give her a cup of tea, and I'll come to see her in the morning."

"I've already given her tea," he lied. "Something upset her at dinnertime and she hasn't been herself since."

"I'll come to see her in half an hour," Blizzard said with mild annoyance.

He did not spend long in the bedroom, and when he came downstairs he looked seriously at the floor.

"I don't know what you did to the girl, but something has upset her badly."

"It wasn't me," Kevin said lamely.

"I'll ring the hospital and ask them to send an ambulance right away. I'm afraid she may be heading for a miscarriage."

He drove behind the ambulance to Portlaoise and sat in the waiting room barely noticing the coming and going of people in the corridor. It was a long night, as long as many a winter, and he had sunk so deeply into himself that the nurse was standing by his side before he looked up at her.

"Your wife's had a baby boy," she said.

"How is she?"

"Very weak, but otherwise as well as can be expected."

"And the boy?"

"He's very small, not four pounds, and we've got him in the incubator."

"Can I see her?"

"She's resting, but you can go in."

She was lying on her back, a face on a pillow, pale as the sheet that was tucked under her chin, the sunken eyes closed as if she had come through death or worse. He stood by the bed, but he could not bring himself to speak in case she should say something he might not want the nurse to hear. After a while the nurse touched his sleeve and he turned and left the ward. In the corridor he met Dr. Blizzard, who took him aside and placed a long-fingered hand on his shoulder.

"We'll have to keep her in for a week or two till she regains her strength."

"What about the boy?"

"He has a fifty-fifty chance. He's as strong as you could expect a baby of his weight to be in the thirtieth week of pregnancy."

In a rush of relief, the tiredness spread from his torso down his arms and legs, not an unpleasant tiredness, more a desire for luxurious relaxation.

"I'll go home now but I'll be back this evening. She was asleep when I went in, and I didn't want to disturb her."

"Will you do me a favour before you go?" Dr. Blizzard asked in his darkest basso profundo. "Will you have a word with Festus O'Flaherty in the next ward? He's just had an operation for a gallstone in the bile duct, and he's convinced that it was for cancer, that he's about to die."

"Well, has he got cancer?"

"No, but he won't believe us doctors. He says that we told the same story to your mother four years ago."

"What can I do?"

"He'll believe you perhaps. You're his friend."

Festus, in a gaudy dressing gown at the far end of the ward, pretended not to see him when he came in the door.

"The first of the vultures come to hover over me," he said. "But I'm not carrion yet, believe me."

"You're looking well."

"The curious thing is that I never felt better. The real pain is gone, but I know it's the end. I'm facing it like a man or, better still, like a mute animal."

"But there's nothing wrong with you."

"Who said that?"

"Blizzard."

"He'd lie to his own mother. He had one of the doctors bring me what he called my gallstone in a jar, but I saw through his little ruse. It was someone else's, not mine."

"Look, Festus, there's nothing the matter with you. You've just said you feel fine."

"Cancer's a treacherous bastard. It retreats for a week only to come back in greater force the next."

"I can see you're not interested in the truth."

"You wouldn't tell me it if I asked you."

"Dying men are supposed to know the truth," said Kevin. "If you don't know it, you can't be dying."

"You're wrong. The only truth a dying man knows is about other people, not himself."

"It's a good beginning."

"Do you want to hear the truth about yourself, Hurley?"

"Only if it can be expressed briefly. The last time a man promised to tell me the truth, it took two hours."

"When was that?"

"At the last mission in Killage. A Redemptorist preacher took two hours to tell us we'd all go to hell."

"I won't keep you two minutes. All I'll say is that you're

inoperable, a terminal case. Your trouble is women, not cancer, but you can't say I didn't warn you."

"Goodbye."

"Before you go, will you make me a promise? Will you see to it that my last words on this earth don't die with me? I've given them some thought. I've honed and polished them, and I want them preserved like gallstones in a jam jar. The only problem now is knowing when to say them."

"What are they?"

"Life is a bowl of filberts and only bitches have nutcrackers. Repeat that till I see if you've got it."

Kevin repeated the famous last words until Festus had satisfied himself that he would not forget them.

"I don't wish to see you again, so go now and don't come back. Standing there on one leg, you remind me of a hooded crow in February waiting for a weak lamb to drop."

Kevin drove back to Clonglass in a state of near euphoria, a reaction from the anxiety in which he had spent the night. Elizabeth was well and the boy was alive, though weak. It had been a close thing. For once White Cloud had not kicked him in the ballocks. He knew that he should be worried about what Elizabeth would say to him when she opened her eyes, but the knowledge that he now had a son and heir was so thrilling that he could think of nothing else.

He did not go to bed but changed into his old clothes and started his round of jobs in the yard. After dinner he went back to Larch Lawn and lay down until it was time to go to see Elizabeth. When he got to the hospital, one of the nurses told him that his wife had spent most of the day asleep, that it almost seemed as if she did not wish to wake up. He did not try to wake her now. He sat by the bed watching her face like a calm lake reflecting the shadows of racing clouds. As he listened to her even breathing, he became aware of how he had come to love her, first from reading her diary while he was ill and then from sensing the grace and goodness in everything she did and said.

Is it now a hopeless love? he asked himself as he got up to go.

The nurse told him that his son was still in the incubator, so he drove home in a more sober and reflective mood than in the morning. In bed he opened her diary and stared for an hour at the entry for December 21st, not knowing what to make of it:

> I am only an interlude in his life, a wife between ploughing and harrowing, between sowing and reaping. The days are dark. Dusk surrounds Kevin on his tractors. He and they are inseparable. He can hardly cross a field without one of his Massey Fergusons. As he drove into the yard at twilight, I thought of Death. As I looked, I saw the macabre austerity of the grille and the sunken headlamps like the empty eyesockets of a skull. Is farming death, and am I half in love with easeful farming?

He must have slept heavily because he could hear a telephone ringing for a long time in his dream before he realized that it was the one in the hallway. He went downstairs in a hurry, prepared for the worst news about the boy.

"Mr. Hurley?" a voice at the other end inquired. "I've got bad news for you, I'm afraid. Your wife has just died. She had a post-partum hemorrhage in the night, and in spite of blood transfusions, she failed to rally."

He drove to the hospital, trying to make sense of "she failed to rally" but incapable of pursuing the simplest thought for one moment at a time. It was a cold morning in the black no man's land between Christmas and the New Year. The fields were frozen, the hedges grey in the headlights, and the flat road unrolled before him like a lonely and desperate life that would never end. He had turned up the heater, but the

227

cold lurked in the lining of his overcoat and between his toes, and the wind that came down from Slieve Bloom in the north blew icy twigs against the windows. He drove quickly as if her life depended on it, as if the cold of the inanimate could yet be beaten into retreat.

"Did she wake up before she died?" he asked the sister on duty.

She looked at him as if he were not quite human, or perhaps not quite shaven, and told him that she had been delirious and confused.

"She kept asking for 'Kevin and the Lad in the Corner.'"

"Kevin is me. Did she say anything else?"

"Before she died, she may have mumbled something about 'Kevin . . . and my last best friend,' but I can't really be sure."

My last best friend. The arresting simplicity of the words almost made him weep. After all he had done to her, she had forgiven him at the end.

The next three days were a nightmare. Neighbours came to the house and consumed large quantities of food and drink, smoked their pipes, and went away. Each morning he rang the hospital to inquire about his son while Elizabeth lay frozen in the coffin upstairs. Twin images struggled for supremacy in his mind during the day and in his dreams at night: the cold corpse in the coffin and the puny body in the warm incubator struggling to retain its grip on life. He came back from the funeral and changed into his old clothes, but as he was pulling on his Wellingtons the telephone rang again.

"It's my son," he cried aloud before picking up the receiver.

He listened without speaking and went into the parlour to sit down. His wife had died, and now his only son and heir. He told himself that it was no more than he had expected in his deeply pessimistic heart. For a single moment he had an intoxicating sense of freedom, of release from the toils of human connection: he felt that he was a man to whom everything except death itself had been done.

He buried his son beside his wife on the last day of the year. Cold and bruised, almost insensible, he drove back from the cemetery in the rain between empty fields and naked hedges. After changing into his farming clothes, he carved himself a plate of beef while Maureen ladled out the sliced turnips and parsnips, the days of baked potatoes with cheese and parsley and parsnips with nutmeg over. He ate in silence, waiting for the steaming food to warm him, while Maureen made sucking noises like a feeding calf. Outside, the daylight was draining away as the misty rain stole in over the hedges. All round were low-lying farms with slushy yards and cattle chewing the cud in contentment. Men were going about their business, carrying buckets of mash that would put flesh and fat on pigs and bullocks. In six weeks would come the first stirrings of spring and a new year in the Grove and fields. Slowly, he peeled a potato and thanked heavens for jobs to be done.

He remembered the day almost a year ago when Maureen told him that she was with child. It had been the most eventful year of his life, and now he was back where he had begun. It was as if for a twelvemonth his life had leant out of the true and had now regained its perpendicularity. Yet that was not correct. He was no longer the man who unthinkingly invited Murt Quane to help him with the shed. He was in debt to Elizabeth if only because she had called him her "last best friend" at the end. He now owed it to her to live in a way that would not horrify her if she were alive. He must somehow ensure that her life and death were not in vain.

"There's a talk about foggage on the radio at four," Maureen said. "Are you going to listen to it?"

"No."

He wished to put distance between himself and his sister, but he could not live at Larch Lawn on his own. He needed the familiar sounds of another human being, eating, breathing, and shuffling about the kitchen. And he needed someone to cook his meals and wash his shirts.

"I've put the hot water bottle in the bed," she said after a while.

"No, Maureen, all that's over."

With all his heart he hoped that it was over. That it wasn't to be like his attempts to give up the pipe. He would go without tobacco for six months, and then a calf would die and he would need the solace of a smoke. He would decide to have just one pipe, and he would not be able to give it up again till the next Lent.

"You're going to listen to the talk about foggage, then?" She placed his bottle of ale before him.

"No, I know more about foggage than anyone else in the country, and with reason."

"What are you going to do, then?"

"I'm going down to Larch Lawn to be quiet for an hour."